I0580602

THE HAUNTED SWORD AND OTHER TALES

JOHN BRICKWEDEL

TABLE OF CONTENTS

1 **THE HAUNTED SWORD**

2 **SMITTY'S RESCUE**

TABLE OF CONTENTS

THE HAUNTED SWORD AND OTHER TALES

Copyright © 2023 by **JOHN BRICKWEDEL**

All rights reserved. No part of this book may be reproduced or transmitted, downloaded, distributed, reverse engineered, or stored in or introduced into any information storage and retrieval system, in any form or by any means, including photocopying and recording, whether electronic or mechanical, now known or hereinafter invented without permission in writing from the publisher.

DISCLAIMER: The contents of this work, including, but not limited to, the accuracy of events, people, and places depicted; opinions expressed; permission to use previously published materials included; and any advice given or actions advocated are solely the responsibility of the author, who assumes all liability for said work and indemnifies the publisher against any claims stemming from publication of the work.

To order additional copies of this book, please contact:

MAPLE LEAF PUBLISHING INC.
www.mapleleafpublishinginc.com

General Inquiries & Customer Service
Phone: 1-(403)-356-0255

Email: info@mapleleafpublishinginc.com

ISBN Paperback: 978-1-77419-212-2

ISBN eBook: 978-1-77419-213-9

THE HAUNTED SWORD

CHAPTER ONE: JOHN

It had been raining for days and we were getting a little bored with our trip to France. To alleviate our boredom, we wandered through the old part of the city, checking out the antique stores. The one we were in had more junk than antiques. My wife, Shannon, was going through all the old clothes and I was looking at the tools, knives, and guns when I came upon a case of old swords. Most of these blades were pretty beat up but the prices were high enough to scare a rich man. There was one with a pretty nice hilt in a fairly elaborate scabbard; the price wasn't bad. Since it was a lot better than most of the rest of them, I was curious as to why it was the most reasonable.

I waved over the old man who worked there and asked him in my bad French why this sword was so cheap. I thought he said that it was haunted but I wasn't sure of the French so I asked him to explain. I had to ask him to slow down a couple of times. He said he had sold the sword many times but the buyer always brought it back. They told him that they were just fine with it until they pulled it out of the scabbard and started waving it around, which one does with a new sword at the first opportunity. When the sword left the scabbard they immediately heard wind whistling and metal clanking, followed by the appearance of a ghost carrying a sword and challenging them to a duel.

I had mixed feelings about purchasing the sword. In the first place I wasn't quite sure that the old man hadn't made up the whole thing just to sell me the sword or to scare me off. He would have a great tale to tell his old buddies at the wine shop the next day about a silly American who ran out of his shop, frightened by a ghost story. On the other hand, if it was true, I had always wanted to see a real live ghost and I had studied fencing with my oldest son; I considered myself pretty good at it.

The longer I thought about it the more excited I got about crossing swords with a ghost. I wandered around the store thinking about it. I decided that if I did buy it I had better not tell my wife about the ghost or I would be in big trouble. I questioned the old man some more. I asked him how you got rid of the ghost if you decided you didn't want to play anymore. He said the ghost would go away if you put the sword back in the scabbard. I also was curious as to whether or not he thought the ghost would go with the sword to America. He thought that was a good question; he wanted me to write and tell him of my adventure. He seemed a little nervous about it, so I told him how good I thought I was with a sword and how I looked forward with great pleasure to an encounter with a ghost. I bought the sword, and almost bought the farm.

We finished our trip around Europe with me lugging the sword around with our baggage. Once settled in at home I was anxious to see if my friend the ghost had followed us and to see if the ghost would talk to me when he appeared. I wanted to know where he came from and why he was haunting the sword. I had to wait until the family left the house to take the sword out to a small clearing in the woods surrounding the house. I looked the ground over carefully and removed any sticks and rocks that might trip me. Then, deciding that I was ready, I pulled the sword from the scabbard, keeping it in my left hand so I could return the sword quickly to the scabbard if the ghost was too good for me.

I stood quietly, anticipating the appearance of my first ghost. Soon I heard a rustling of leaves as a wind gust came from the other side of the clearing, then a sound like that of armor rattling together. Then a short man dressed like one of the Three Musketeers came out of the trees carrying a sword in his hand. He stopped in the middle of the clearing and looked me over for a minute, then went into the guard position. Awestruck, I just stood there staring until, to my great surprise, he spoke. "En guard!" he commanded in French.

"Wait! Don't you think we should introduce ourselves before you try to kill me? Besides, you have an unfair advantage. It is possible for you to kill me but quite impossible for me to kill a Ghost."

He lunged. I had hoped that his ghostly blade would be only vapor as I was sure the ghost was, but it was not so. My blade parried his thrust and flicked back to knock the plumed hat from his head. Then he jumped back and pointed his blade at the ground, and asked, "What do you mean 'ghost'?" I lowered my sword.

"The fact that you are floating about a foot off the ground might give you some clue." He looked at his feet, and lowered himself to the ground.

"Now you have the advantage of height," he protested.

"My name is John Brix. I don't even know you. Why are you here attacking me?" He lunged again. This time the battle went on for a number of minutes before he stepped back and again lowered his sword.

"I am here," he said, "because at some time in the past I was stabbed in the back with that sword. And I am here to avenge myself."

"Can't you tell by my clothes and appearance that I am not from your time in history?" I asked. He looked me over for a minute. "You do look a bit strange, and your accent is very bad too." Again I asked, "What is your name, and where are you from?"

"My name is Pierre de Martinprey, and I am from Animass France. Now, en guard."

So we went back to our fight. He had no great advantage over me, even though you could tell that he had had a lot of experience with the sword. His movements were a little slow. That could be from many years of inactivity, or maybe just old age. As I pondered these things, he suddenly jumped back and said, "Brix. I know that name. It is from Normandy on the coast."

"I am from the Danish branch of the family," I responded. "What year were you born?"

"Sixteen sixty-four. What year is it now?"

"Nineteen ninety-six."

"What kind of fool do you think I am? Would you have me believe that I am nigh unto 340 years old?" Just then we heard a car coming up the road. He demanded, "What in the name of all the saints is that noise?"

"It's a car, and that must be my wife coming home."

"I would like to see this." He turned and went through the trees until he could see the car in front of the garage and my wife getting out. I had followed him from the woods, and was standing beside him when the thought came to me that it might not be too fine an idea for my wife to see Pierre le Ghost. Shannon is from good Irish stock and very excitable, so I slid the sword back into the scabbard and he vanished. My sword arm was tired and I was glad that the fight was over for now, but promised myself that we would fight another day.

I waited until my wife went into the house before I left the woods. I stopped in the garage and put the sword up in the rafters so the kids wouldn't get it. When I went into the kitchen my wife asked, "What happened to your arm?" I looked at my shirtsleeve. It was slit and was soaked with blood. I rolled the sleeve up and there was a huge gash halfway up my forearm. It may have been only an inch long but it was bleeding some. I told my wife that I had been out in the woods and probably scraped it on something. As I cleaned it up and bandaged it, I knew the blade that had made the wound was not made of phantom mists. I was just glad it hadn't been run through me.

Over the next few weeks I was too busy in my construction business to have another go around with friend ghost but, while I worked, I thought about what had happened; I was not certain that it was not just a figment of my imagination but then I would look at the scar on my arm and decide it must be real. To tell the truth, I have to admit that I was a little afraid of the ghost. Not because he was a ghost. He wasn't even scary. He was actually a little comical, not very spooky for a spook. The cut on my arm was proof that his blade could cut me and that it could kill me. Sword fighting with razor sharp blades with a guy who has no fear because he cannot die because he is already dead is akin to insanity. But it wasn't insanity that finally took me back to the clearing in the woods. It was curiosity. A hundred questions kept coming into my mind such as did he follow the sword on his own, or did the sword somehow have the power to draw him along with it wherever it went? And so on. I thought I would see what I could find out about him on my own, so I went to the computer. I didn't find much. There is not much information about the sixteen hundreds in the computer.

The first time the family was away for the day I found myself with sword in hand, back at the clearing. I composed myself for the fight, and drew the sword. Just like before, first came the wind and then the clanking, and then Pierre le Ghost. He walked to the center of the clearing and stopped. He looked his usual self: blank stare, dusty clothes, and sword. He went to the guard position, and at his "En guard," we fell to. After a few minutes of slashing and stabbing I stepped back and dropped the point of my sword to the ground, showing I wanted a break. I asked him if he was somehow forced to follow the sword. He responded, "I don't know. I'm just here."

"Even though this was the sword that stabbed you in the back, you must realize that I'm not the one who did it."

"Yes."

"The person who stabbed you has been dead for three hundred years. Must you go on attacking anyone who draws this blade forever?"

"I feel compelled to do so until I have been avenged. Now: en guard!"

He attacked with a will, but I was never one to give ground, so with great fury the blades flashed in the sun, sparks flying with the power of the strokes. After about five minutes of this he stepped back and dropped the point of his blade; when I responded by dropping mine, he lunged. His movements were a little slow, allowing me to jump aside and slash down with an angry swing. His blade broke.

We both stood and stared at the hilt and the broken stump of a blade in his hand. When he dropped the point of his sword, he had asked for a break in the battle. To then lunge was to cheat. This ghost was cheating.

"Is this a demonstration of the honor of a Gentleman of France?" I demanded. He glared at me but said nothing. I picked up the sheath for my sword, while watching him out of the comer of my eye, and said, "I am tempted to sheath this cursed blade and cast it into the sea, so I never have to look at your cowardly face again." His face changed from an angry expression to one of shock. "Please, I apologize," he stammered. Being too angry to listen, I slid the sword back into its case, and he faded away. I looked at the ground to see if his broken blade was there but it too was gone.

As I walked back to the house I decided to put the sword up and not to take any more chances with Old Spooky's honor. I went straight to my shop, which was seldom invaded by anyone in the family other than my wife borrowing a tool that never seemed to get returned. I put the sword up in the rafters with some old camping gear. I thought it would be safe there. I was pretty angry with Pierre, so I didn't go back to the clearing for a while. However, I was intrigued by his treachery and determined to find its explanation so I did finally return to the clearing, drew my sword, and wait for him. My musty Musketeer didn't go right to the guard position, but walked to the center of the clearing, dropped the tip of his sword, and bowed slightly. He said, "I apologize for my behavior at our last meeting. I am very glad to see that you did not destroy your sword and I am glad to see you again."

"But why did you do it?"

"It was just a sudden urge. I will try to control myself in the future, if you care to carry on."

"All right then. En guard."

Over the next year or so, Pierre and I met in the woods periodically for a little swordplay and conversation until one day he became frustrated because he was not doing well and tried another sneaky trick, in response to which I conked him on the head with the flat of my sword. He stepped back, dropped the tip of his sword, and said, "I know that you could kill me anytime that you want. Why haven't you?"

"I enjoy the fight and besides you're already a ghost. I don't know what would happen if I chopped off your arm. Would you have a new one when you came back, like you had a new blade? Or would that end it all?"

He just stared at me for a few moments, bowed his head and said, "I don't know the answer to your questions." I saluted with my sword, bid him adieu, put the sword in the scabbard, and returned it to the hiding place in the rafters.

A few months later, while reading peacefully in the living room, I heard a lot of scuffling, yelling, and screaming coming from the family room directly below me. I ran down the stairs to see my ten year old daughter in one comer of the room doing the screaming, while her fifteen year old brother was lying on his back on the floor with the ghost standing over him with his sword point at my son's throat.

My son must have found the sword in the shop and brought it in to show his sister. When he pulled the blade from the sheath, Pierre appeared. When he ran from the ghost, he dropped the blade, which lay on the floor near me. I picked it up. The movement got the attention of the ghost, who quickly turned to face me. I muttered, "Just to keep this from going any farther, I'll put this up." Watching him all the time, I picked up the sheath and backed out the door into the garage. I kept backing through the garage into the driveway with His Dustiness following and the two frightened kids watching from the door.

Without warning, he attacked. We fought for a few minutes, swords clashing and flashing in the sun. He lunged high. I knocked his blade aside, swung my blade in an arc, and brought it down hard, hoping to again break his sword, but it was only knocked from his hand. He moved forward to pick it up, but I stepped on it, and put the point of my blade against his chest. The tip was actually pushing in on the dusty old material of his vest so I figured I could do some damage to old Pierre even if I couldn't kill him again.

"I don't know what to do about you now that the kids know about you. They will surely tell their mother, and I'll have to do something about it." He looked back at the kids still hovering in the doorway.

"They look old enough to watch gentlemen fight a duel of honor."

"You are not a gentleman. You are just a dusty old replica of one and a cheat."

"Let me have my sword and I will have your blood for saying that."

I stepped back and away from his sword. As he bent to pick it up I slid my blade back into its sheath, and he faded away. I looked down the driveway to see if there were any cars on the country lane but the road was empty. A glance at the house revealed two kids frozen in the doorway. I went to the shop, got a ladder, and put the sword back.

I marched into the house with the kids in tow, sat them down, told them the whole story, and warned them that no one would believe them if they told what had happened. Furthermore, if they got the sword down to prove that they weren't making it all up, old Pierre might kill them. They assured me that they had seen enough to be too afraid to go near that sword again.

The next big scene came when my wife got home. I thought I had better tell her about Pierre before she got the story from the kids. As soon as she came in I sat her down and told the story again, including what had happened to the kids, leaving out my close shaves and the other scary parts. At first she didn't believe it, but after questioning me and the kids, she decided I might be telling the truth. She turned to face me and growled, "Get rid of it. I won't have something that dangerous around the house. What kind of an idiot takes such chances with his life, anyway?" I told her that getting rid of it would not be easy. I explained that throwing it in the lake or burying it was dangerous because if anyone found it and didn't know how to handle a sword they might be killed. We discussed the problem for a while, and decided that we would buy a gun safe, lock it up, and throw away the key.

I was a bit reluctant to get rid of the sword so it sat in the attic until the day I decided to call my oldest son, Eric, and tell him what had transpired. I couldn't think of a good way to break the story to him so I just told him to bring his son, Ryan, and his sister's son, Cody, and come for a visit. Eric and I had taken fencing lessons for two years when he was 18 and 19 so I was sure he would be very interested. They arrived the next weekend and I sat them all down and told them the whole story. They were all pretty skeptical even though my younger son, Rick, and younger daughter, Mallory, swore that I was telling the truth. We discussed the problems with getting rid of the sword. When asked for his advice, he said, "Dad, I am a long way from convinced that this is not one of your elaborate practical jokes. Put on a demonstration for us, Pop, and we will all be convinced. Until I see this spook for myself, I refuse to get embroiled in another of your pranks." I thought about it for a minute, then acquiesced, "Okay, Eric, but everybody must stay completely out of sight. I don't know what he might do if he saw any of you."

I went to the shop and got the old sword down and we all walked out to the clearing in the woods. I warned them to be very quiet and to hide in the brush around the clearing on the side away from Pierre's usual entry point. When they were concealed, I drew the blade from the sheath but kept the sheath in my hand in case I needed it. In the usual order, there was a gust of wind, the rattle of armor, and out strolled old Pierre le Ghost.

He got into the guard position and roared, "En guard."

The day was clear and the sun flashing off our blades almost blinded our audience. For some reason he was in a real fighting mood. He lunged; I knocked his sword aside and, before he could withdraw, I skewered his hat and flipped it from his head. We fought for about five minutes--I wasn't watching the clock-- then I stepped back and lowered my blade; so did he. I asked, "Since you pretty well shook up my family the last time you came around, how would you like to meet some of them?" He bowed slightly, "It would be a great honor to meet the family of my opponent. You have fought like a true gentleman, and I would very much like to meet them."

Keeping the sheath in hand, I called, "All you boys can come out. My two sons, Eric and Rick, came out; then, more cautiously, the two grandsons, Cody and Ryan, came out. I was keeping a pretty close watch on old Pierre to make sure he didn't try anything funny, but he just bowed to them and tucked his sword under his left arm. So I introduced them to him in French and him to them in English. He asked the boy's ages and if they had had any training with the sword. I told him their ages and that Eric had had some lessons "and a lot of practice with his old Papa."

"And the others?"

"It is not common today for men to settle their differences with a sword. It is just not done anymore."

During our conversation my wife and younger daughter had come out of hiding, so I introduced them to Old Dusty and told everybody in English what we had been saying in French. Then there was a long question and answer session, necessitating my services as translator, stretching my vocabulary and overheating my brain. "It is time we discuss what to do about this." I started to put the blade and the old spook away when Eric spoke up. "Wait, Dad. This has a lot to do with the old ghost. Why not let him help in the decision?"

While we were talking old Pierre had stooped to pick up his hat and replace it on his head. Once again properly attired, he demanded to know, "What is all the talk about that you so rudely leave me out of?"

"The family would like to know if you could stop trying to kill anybody who pulls this sword out of its sheath."

He turned to the family, removed his hat, and with an elaborate bow said, "I am afraid not. There seems to be some kind of curse on the sword and I have no idea how to break it." While translating his response, I slid the sword back into the scabbard, and old Mr. Spook faded away.

As we walked back to the house the kids babbled their excitement at seeing a ghost in swordplay with their grandfather. The adults were quiet; Shannon was thinking about the ghost and I was thinking about how much trouble I was in with Shannon. Once we were all seated around the family room, the kids around the stone hearth and Eric and Shannon on the couch, I stood with my back to the TV and opened the discussion. "Now that we have seen Mr. Ghost I think we can agree that he is a menace to the safety of this family and needs to be done away with."

"No, Grandpa, he was real neat!" my two grandsons yelled in unison. Cody, the older of the two, said, "Come on, Grandpa, this is the first time anybody we know has ever seen a ghost, and besides, you weren't having any trouble with him. You're really good with that sword."

At this point, my lovely wife spoke up. "Yes, Cody, we all know that your grandpa can do no wrong, and that he is a good swordsman, but that doesn't mean the rest of us are. Ask Rick. He still hasn't gotten over his encounter with the ghost. What a shocking experience! To have a ghost appear, knock the sword from your hand, and almost run you through would be enough to give an older person a heart attack. Without any fooling around, we need to get rid of that sword. I cannot believe, John, that you would endanger yourself and the rest of us with such a threat." Eric, who is a big, quiet guy, said, "You have to understand, Shannon, that once Dad had told everyone not to touch that sword, he would expect everybody to leave it be, like his loaded guns around the house."

"Yeah, but nobody knew the sword was loaded."

"Well he couldn't very well tell anyone, could he?"

"You sound like you agree with what he did. I can't believe this."

"I may not agree with what he did, but, being his son, I can understand his excitement and curiosity when the shopkeeper told him the story of the sword. In his place, I probably would have done the same thing if I had had the guts to try."

Shannon retorted, "Yeah, you're a chip off the old block, but not quite as demented."

Demented? "Thanks, gang, for all the compliments, but that's all water under the bridge. We need to decide the fate of the sword."

My wife said, "I think we should go to Seattle and drop it in the deepest part of the sound to let the sea rust it away. Then it will be gone forever."

"That would probably work. Then all we would have to worry about is some poor fisherman snagging it and finding out by accident about the curse. No, I think we should buy a gun safe and lock it up and through away the key."

"Oh, sure, but you would keep a spare key and when no one was home you would be out in the woods playing with your friend again."

After a few minutes of silence, Eric announced his decision. "Shannon is probably right. I will take it out in my boat when I get home and dispose of it." While the children and grandchildren invented ways to get rid of friend spook, I headed for the garage to return the sword to its hiding place. When I returned, Eric was still sitting where he had been; he appeared to be thinking, which is not a normal thing for him and always worries me a little. The two grandsons were taking turns trying to talk my wife into keeping the spook. They were not getting anywhere. The rest of the day and night everyone was pretty glum, except Shannon. She was relieved and was extra sweet, trying to cheer everyone up.

The next day was another beautiful day in the Idaho panhandle, a great day for grandpa to have a farewell fight with Mr. Pierre le Spook, or so the grandsons argued, but Shannon said no so Eric took the sword and the boys and left for home, promising to send us a video of the commitment of the poor old sword to a watery grave. Shannon was happy with that; I was not. That ghost had provided me with a wonderful way to vent my frustrations in much the same way that a golfer takes his frustrations out on a defenseless little golf ball. It was also very exciting, like skiing and racing downhill on an icy mountain. If you are not living on the edge, you are not having much fun. With the ghost gone, the fun was over and life seemed a little empty. Ten days later, we received in the mail the dreaded video. It showed Eric and the boys out on their boat, making a great production of deep-sixing the sword.

Life goes on. For a few weeks things went along as usual; then Eric called. My daughter Mallory answered the phone. I could tell who was calling by the way she talked to him. I really wasn't in the mood to talk to him but when Mal handed me the phone, I took it.

"Hello, son."

"Hi, Pop. Mallory said you were still feeling down

about us dumping the blade in the drink, but I have a Cheerer-Upper for you. Why don't you come over for a few days and we'll take the boat out for some fishing? The salmon are hitting big just out around the point. Besides, Cody and Ryan have something they are all excited about showing you."

"What?"

"I'm not supposed to tell you, but it is really special. You better get your rear end in your rig and get over here."

"Oh, okay. I'll be over this weekend."

"Good. Come Friday night so we can go out fishing early on Saturday."

"Okay. I'll see you Friday." I hung up the phone.

The drive over the mountains on Friday afternoon was beautiful. It was the end of summer and the weather was great, not a cloud in the sky. I was feeling pretty good; I had a premonition that something good was going to happen. Maybe the fish were going to be biting, but probably not. Not with my luck.

When I pulled into Eric's driveway, my older daughter, Sonja, came out of the house, a stampede of granddaughters right behind her. Haley, Ellen, and Mariah were all yelling, "Grandpa, Grandpa." While I was giving everyone a hug, Haley, the oldest, informed me, "The boys are out back practicing. Come, Grandpa, and see what they're doing." Ellen, who is four, echoed, "Come, Grandpa," and grabbed my hand. Mariah took the other one and they pulled me around to the back of the house.

The boys were waiting, all dressed in fencing gear, with swords in their hands. Cody welcomed me with, "Hi Grandpa. Watch and see how well we are doing." They went right to work, moving back and forth with swords clashing. As I watched the boys, I walked over by Eric and said, "They look pretty good. You must have spent a lot of time practicing with them:"

"Yeah, but they have been working very hard. They want to get good enough to fight old Pierre." I whirled to face him and growled, "Yeah, sure, if the old sword wasn't sleeping at thirty fathoms in Davy Jones' locker." Unnoticed, Sonja and the three granddaughters had joined us. Sonja asked, "Who is Pierre?"

The two boys stopped their grand display of arms, walked over to us, and with great energy and excitement began to educate their aunt. "Pierre is the old Frenchman Grandpa was sword fighting with," said Ryan. "It was really neat. You should have seen it, Aunt Sonja."

"What is going on, Dad? I didn't think you had touched a sword in a long time."

"Oh, an old French gentleman and I have been doing a little fencing for the last couple of years, and I let them watch us while they were there last month. I suppose that's the reason for the sudden interest."

Eric jumped in to rescue me, "Yeah, as soon as we got back from your place they made me dig out the old sabers and teach them how to use them. Let's go in the house. It must be about lunch time and I'm starved after watching all this exercise."

Once we were in the house the kids went to wash up for lunch and Sonja went to the kitchen to talk to Eric's wife, Andrea, leaving us alone for a few minutes. I challenged him, "So you faked the dumping of the sword. Why?"

"On the way back from your place the boys and I decided that we would like to have a go at the old ghost ourselves so we worked out a plan to fool Shannon, so her mind would be at rest, and went to work practicing."

"As I remember, you weren't bad with the sword back when we were taking lessons, but that was a long time ago. You and I had better do some practicing, so I can show you Old Spooky's favorite moves."

"I noticed when you were fighting the old guy that you were careful not to hurt him. You knocked his hat off and such, but you didn't touch him. Why is that?"

"Well, I'm not sure what would happen. If I chopped something off it might not grow back. That might stop all my fun. I could have run him through every time we fought, but the bosses of spook land may cut him off, telling him that he had had his chance, and then I'd never see him again. I've questioned him but he doesn't know what would happen either so I don't take any chances."

About then Andrea called us for lunch. After lunch we went outside, and took up the fencing sabers and practiced until our arms were tired. While we were taking a break I lectured my son and grandsons. "You know the old guy is not fooling around. He is out for blood and revenge. Someone could get hurt. If that happened, Shannon would have my rear end. That old ghost may be a little slow in his movements, but he knows every trick in the book." Eric sarcastically chanted, "Yes, Daddy. I'll be careful, Daddy," which caused the lecture to intensify. "I know it might have looked easy but it is not. You are not as experienced as I am so, for your family's sake, don't try it alone. At least have one of the boys there in case you get hurt. He can distract Pierre until you can sheath the sword, so he can't kill you."

"Okay, Dad, I'll be careful. How about if you come

over whenever we want to give it a try? Then both you and I will feel better about it?"

"Yeah," I agreed, "he sometimes asks questions, and you don't speak the lingo." We went back to working out with the swords for a while longer, and I showed Eric some of the old spooks favorite tricks. Early the next day we went fishing and, even though we each caught some fish, the conversation while fishing was all about fighting ghosts. After dinner that night, Eric said, "I am really looking forward to trying my hand with the Frenchman. I have the perfect spot for it in the woods just down the street from my house. How about we do it before the family is up, at first light tomorrow morning?"

"Alright, Eric but you have to remember that this is no game to him. He means business." There was no opportunity for further discussion and instruction. Three little granddaughters drug their grandfather off to play games with them in the play room. I didn't sleep very well that night. I kept thinking about the dangers of someone seeing us out there in the woods. I decided to talk to Eric about it in the morning and finally fell asleep.

The sun has a habit of coming up even when you don't want it to; however, that hadn't happened yet when Eric came to get me. The grandsons, Cody and Ryan, were making a lot of noise trying to be quiet, bubbling over with excitement. I whispered, "Boys, be quiet. If you wake up the females in this house, we won't be able to do this." They both put fingers to their lips, signaling silence, and we all crept quietly out the basement door. We walked down through the woods behind the house about six hundred yards until we came to the place that Eric thought would be secure enough for his duel with friend Pierre.

Trying one last time to talk him out of it, I said, "This is crazy, Eric. There are houses all around. If someone should come upon us while we're doing this, well, the shit could hit the fan." He argued, "It's early, Dad, nobody is going to be around when it's barely daylight." While Eric and the boys picked up things that might be tripped over I searched the area in a wide circle to see if any houses or people might be close enough to see or hear the fight. The trees were thick enough to provide excellent cover. I saw no houses or people. When I returned to the clearing, Eric called out, "Where have you been? We're ready."

"Wait a second. Cody, you go down that way, where you can still see but can look around. If you see anyone, sing out so we can get rid of Pierre before someone sees him. Ryan, you go up that way and watch." They grumbled, but they went. When I was satisfied that they were in position, I signaled Eric. With a great flourish, he drew the sword. After the wind and the rattle of armor, out strolled Pierre. Instead of going into his usual en garde position, he stopped, looked at Eric, then looked at me, and said in French, "Why is your son holding the sword, instead of you?" I replied, "After witnessing our last bout he thought it would be a great honor to test his skill against such a great swordsman as you." He tucked his sword under his arm, took off his hat, bowed first to me and then to Eric. "The honor will be all mine."

Eric saluted with his sword, and went into the guard position. Pierre took his position, called, "En garde," and attacked. As the sun came up over the mountains to the east, it cast its light on a strange scene in the little clearing in the woods. Eric was six feet, two inches and weighed two hundred and sixty pounds. The ghost was short and skinny. To make up for the height difference, Pierre was staying about a foot off the ground. I watched the two closely to see who had the advantage, but I could see none. They attacked and counter attacked, fighting hard for about five minutes, then Pierre stepped back and dropped the tip of his sword. When Eric did the same, Pierre turned to me, "Your son fights well, and has great strength, but he is not as good as you. Your sword moves like a serpent's tongue. His moves like a Viking battle axe." I translated only the first part of that; I didn't want Eric to chop Pierre into little chunks.

CHAPTER TWO: CODY

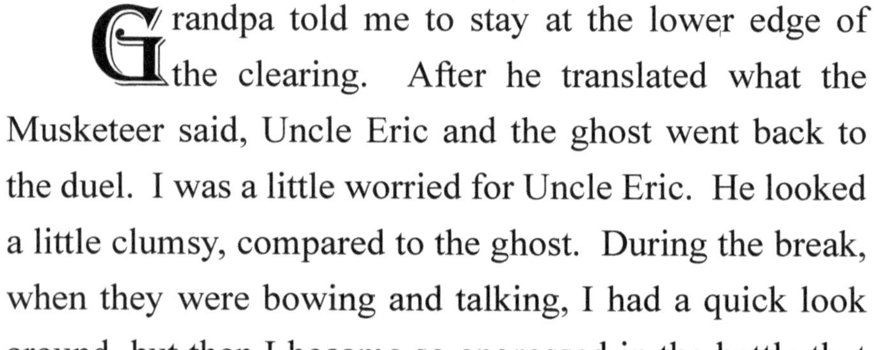

Grandpa told me to stay at the lower edge of the clearing. After he translated what the Musketeer said, Uncle Eric and the ghost went back to the duel. I was a little worried for Uncle Eric. He looked a little clumsy, compared to the ghost. During the break, when they were bowing and talking, I had a quick look around, but then I became so engrossed in the battle that I didn't hear anybody come up behind me until a voice said, "Wow, Cody, that is really cool."

I let out a yell that alerted everybody. Uncle Eric and Pierre dropped their sword tips and turned to look at the

again, we get to watch." Uncle Eric and Grandpa walked off a ways and talked quietly for a few minutes. When they came back Uncle Eric said, "All right but, like Dad told you, it's very important for you not to say anything about this." Uncle Eric is big, like the Hulk, with a deep voice, so when he looks down at you and says to keep your mouth shut, it makes an impression. The girls looked a little scared. I'm sure they would have sworn to anything at that moment. Since I was head over heels in love with Maggie, I felt it was my duty to jump to her defense. I stepped up beside her. "It is okay, Uncle Eric, they won't say anything. We have known them a long time; they are our friends." Uncle Eric warned them one more time not to say anything, then Grandpa and he went back to his house, leaving the sisters and Ryan and me in the clearing. Maggie turned to me, "Wow, Cody, that was scary but exciting, too. Have you fought the ghost yet?" Maggie was actually talking to me; she never had before. "Not yet. I have only practiced with Uncle Eric and Ryan. Grandpa says that I will have to work with him so that I can learn all the tricks that old Pierre uses so that I don't get killed."

Shelley said, "Oh yeah, the curse. That is all still a little hard to believe." Ryan spoke up then, "Ask Grandpa to show you the scar on his arm where old Pierre slashed him in their first battle." About that time the girls' mom called for them so they headed for home and so did we. As I walked, I vowed that I would work hard practicing with Grandpa, so that I could be a big hero to Maggie by fighting the Ghost.

When we got back to the house, Ryan and I went to find Grandpa; Aunt Andrea said he was in the play room with Uncle Eric. As I got near to the play room, I could hear that they were not playing anything, but were talking urgently in low tones. I stayed in the hall, out of sight, and listened. Grandpa was talking. "I was doing this thing with old Pierre for two years without anything going wrong. Now look at it; we have just about the whole family in on it, plus a couple of teenage female blabbermouths."

"What are you so worried about, Dad? Like you said, we just refuse to bring Pierre out, and nobody can prove anything."

"You had better lock up the sword somewhere so no kid gets to it by accident."

"You're right, Pop. We don't want the same thing happening here that happened to Rick at your house. I'll lock it in the gun cabinet." Uncle Eric picked up the sword; Grandpa started toward me so I strolled around the corner natural like and said, "Grandpa, I have been looking for you. Before you head back, will you do a little fencing with me? I want to learn how to manage the tricks Old Pierre uses."

"Well, since I have to leave this afternoon and I won't be back for a while, I guess so, but do you mind if I eat breakfast first? I'm hungry."

After breakfast, Grandpa and I went out to the back yard and started practicing with the fencing sabers. I was working real hard at it because if I was ever going to impress Maggie I had to be good enough to fight the old Frenchman. Grandpa stepped back, dropped the tip of his sword, and nodded his head toward something behind me. I turned around; Maggie and Shelley were there at the end of the yard watching us.

"We came to talk to you, Cody's Grandpa," Shelley said. "We have to call you that since we don't know your name." I cut in with, "His name is John Brix."

"Well, it is nice to meet you, Mr. Brix." Maggie chimed in. "We know you don't live around here, and we're very excited about seeing . . .".

"Old Pierre?" Grandpa said, finishing her sentence for her. We walked over to the girls. Grandpa lowered his voice, "We call him Pierre, or Old Pierre, or the Frenchman, but we don't ever mention the word 'ghost.' He is just an old Frenchman we are taking some fencing lessons from. What if one of those checkout stand magazines found out about this? We would be in trouble and, if my wife found out that Eric didn't throw the old sword in the drink, she would be over here in a minute, and the boys and I would all be roasting on a spit."

"We promised we would be quiet about it, Mr. Brix, and we will but we would like to know when you are coming over again so we can be here to watch the 'fencing lessons' again."

"It will be about a month. Cody will let you know, won't you Cody?" To myself I whispered, "You ornery old coot!" but out loud I almost shouted, "Yes, sir." Grandpa had already figured out that I was crazy about Maggie and I could tell he had plans to give me a bad time about it. I looked at her standing there in her white shorts and red tee shirt with her long pony tail swinging between her shoulder blades. How could anyone not be in love with her? I was pretty sure she didn't know how I felt about her though, and I didn't want her to find out through Grandpa's teasing. To try to cover up a little I promised her, "I'll get your number from Uncle Eric and call you as soon as I hear from Grandpa."

In an attempt to get Grandpa away from Maggie so he wouldn't give me away, I grabbed him by the arm, turned him toward Uncle Eric and pleaded, "Come on. Let's get some more practicing in before you have to leave for home." We walked back to the clearing and went back to work. I was concentrating real hard, trying to learn as much as I could from Grandpa while he was here because he didn't come over very often. Suddenly, he stepped back, dropped the tip of his sword, and pointed over my shoulder with his chin. I turned and looked behind me. Maggie and Shelley had walked up and were watching. Maggie said, "You guys are good." Shelley asked, "Yeah, but who is the best?" Just to clarify the situation I jumped in with, "Grandpa is the best." Uncle Eric and Pierre are about even, and I'm better than Ryan." Grandpa cut in with, "Pierre knows every trick in the book and he is real smooth, but his movements are a little slow so Eric can handle him, but just barely. Cody is doing well, though. It won't be long before he passes Eric and me."

That was high praise, coming from Grandpa, but only I knew he was saying that to tease me in front of Maggie. I looked at her; she smiled, "Well, Cody, if your grandpa is the best, and you are getting better than the rest, it doesn't look like it will be long before you can fight the, uh, I mean Pierre, right?" Grandpa agreed, "Yes, ma' am, he will soon be the champ." I cut in quickly, knowing he was once again trying to embarrass me, "Yeah, but it will take a while because I don't get to work with Grandpa often enough, and Uncle Eric isn't a good teacher." Maggie looked wistful and begged, "When you come over on the weekend to practice with Eric and Ryan, could you teach me how to do it, too?" Shelley chimed in with, "Me too. It looks like fun." Grandpa smiled real big, but at least he didn't make any wise cracks. I said, "Great idea! We could start after lunch." Grandpa made a little bow. "It would be my pleasure to teach you how to fence, and speaking of lunch, I think I'll go see if Andrea has it ready yet." With a big grin on his face, he took off his glove, handed it and his sword to me, and went in the house. I was glad he was leaving. He can be such a jerk sometimes.

I showed the girls some of the basic fencing positions then I took over as teacher and we worked for about an hour. Since instructing Maggie involved standing behind her, reaching around her, taking hold of her wrist to show her how to move the sword in the guard positions, and just touching her like that, it was wonderful. Her sister Shelley didn't seem to need as much help as Maggie did. Shelley asked if she could practice without the masks as they were messing up her hair. I told her that Uncle Eric would put up the swords if he saw her practicing without masks. She argued that Eric and Pierre were using real swords and they weren't using masks.

"Those guys are not training. Grandpa and Uncle Eric are good swordsmen, and they can handle the Frenchman, but he means business. He is out to kill whoever draws that sword."

"That's crazy. Why would you want to fight someone that you can't kill, when he is trying to kill you? I can't wait until I'm good enough to try it myself."

"It does seem crazy," Maggie said, "but I suppose it's no different from boxing or dirt bike racing."

Now I admit that it may have been my wishful thinking, but I'm sure the way she was looking at me was pure hero worship. There was adoration in those beautiful green eyes. I put up the fencing equipment and walked the girls home. By then Grandpa was ready to leave.

As he drove off, while we were still standing in the street waving goodbye, Uncle Eric asked, "So how long have you been in love with Margaret?" My nasty kinsman, Ryan, butted in with, "Ever since she started growing boobs."

"Thanks, cuz, but I'm not admitting anything." As we walked back to the house, Uncle Eric grinned, "You don't have to."

One night a week, and every Saturday for the next few weeks I got someone to drive me over to Uncle Eric's house to practice. It wasn't as hard to get someone to drive me over there as it was to get Uncle Eric to practice with me. He would always say, "Cody, I have to work. I can't just come home and play swords with you any time you want just so you can impress your girlfriend." But we managed to get in an hour or two every time I could get over there. The girls came over every Saturday; Ryan and I would work with them until Uncle Eric got home. He grumbled all the time we were practicing, like, "I work all day, Cody, and you make me do this when I get home." And I would say, "Quit crying. You need to work off some of that fat anyway." That would get me a whack with side of his saber on my leg or some other exposed body part. What a meanie!

On the second Saturday, while I was working with the girls, Maggie asked, "Why are you working so hard at this, Cody?" Ryan, who was sitting in a lawn chair watching, said, "Just so he can be here with you."

"Ryan, you pea brain!" When I turned and started

toward him with a saber in my hand, he took off running and laughing like a fool. When I turned back both girls were smiling. Shelley said, "Don't worry, Cody, we all know. Besides, she likes you too." I know my face was red but when I looked at Maggie she just smiled at me. Wow! Right then I thought I knew what Heaven will be like. I gave the saber back to Maggie and the two girls went back to fencing. No more teaching; I just watched Maggie. I don't think I could have said anything instructive anyway because my mind was stuck on only one thought: she likes me too. After that, things changed. When we were alone, we held hands, and once she asked me to kiss her. That was scary but after a little of her good instruction, I developed more confidence--and skill.

Grandpa finally showed up one Saturday, and we went right to work with the swords, first he and Uncle Eric dueling and then Grandpa and me. It seemed funny that he, being as old as dirt, could work with both of us, one after the other, but he didn't seem to tire out. He wasn't as big as Uncle Eric, but he seemed to be just as strong.

The girls showed up while Grandpa and I were still going at it. Because they were watching, I put on a real show for a few minutes. I finally stepped back, dropped the tip of my sword, saluted Grandpa, took off my mask, walked over to Maggie and, with my usual grace, charm, and originality said, "Hi."

"Hi. Wow! You are really doing great. You look about ready."

"Nope, not yet."

Shelley argued, "You were looking pretty good. It got me all excited, watching your blade flashing in the sun. It looked like your grandpa was about ready to drop his sword and run." Everybody laughed. Grandpa had to join in with, "I was about ready to run. I had been falling asleep out there until you showed up, then it looked like he was possessed by a devil. It really scared me."

And I have to take this in front of my whole family; even the little girls were giggling. I must have been red all over. Maggie came to my rescue, "You looked great, Cody. You guys quit picking on him." About then Aunt Andrea came out on the deck and said that dinner was ready, "Shelley, I called your mom. She said it was all right for you and Maggie to stay for dinner if you want to. You know, in honor of Cody's grandpa being here." She said that last part with a smirk. Shelley laughed and said, "Yes, we'll stay, in Grandpa's honor."

Maggie and I took all the fencing gear to the garage

to put it up, while everybody else went in the house. When we were alone Maggie asked, "Those two are always teasing you. Does it bother you?"

"No, because it's about us. It makes me feel real proud because I, I, I love you." I stammered and blushed but she came and put her arms around my neck. I put my arms around her, and we kissed our very best kiss so far.

The next morning at just about daylight, we were all out in the woods ready for another battle with old Mr. Ghost. Uncle Eric had the big sword, and Grandpa and I each had one of the fencing swords just in case someone showed up and we needed to put on a good show while Eric made Pierre disappear. It was grandpa's idea; I thought it unnecessary. Who would be stupid enough to be out in these moldy old woods at dawn anyway, other than us, of course?

When everybody was ready and we had all taken our places around the clearing, Eric drew the sword. In the usual order, we heard the wind, the clanking armor, and watched the arrival of Pierre le Ghost. Now that was the scary part; the hair stood up on the back of my neck. Maggie grabbed my arm and Shelley stepped around behind us. Before Pierre went into the guard position, he looked around at all of us, and said something in French to Grandpa, who answered him in French. Pierre looked again at the girls, which made Maggie clamp down harder on my arm, then he said to Eric, "En guard," and they went at it. Grandpa always said that the old spook was a little slow in his movements but those swords were flicking in and out, up and down and around so fast that you could hardly follow it with your eyes. Eric was pretty much staying in one place, but Pierre was circling back and forth. Eric had to jump back quickly to keep from getting stuck, but as he jumped he also struck down hard with his blade and knocked the sword out of Pierre's hand. Eric stood for a second with the point of his blade against Pierre's chest then he stepped back and lowered his tip. Pierre turned and walked over to Grandpa; they held a long conversation in French, which Grandpa translated, "Pierre says that you are very strong, Eric, and that if you had the finesse of your father you would be unbeatable. And he said that, if we had lived in his day, with our sword arms alone, we could have carved out a kingdom for ourselves. When he first appeared, he wanted to know who the girls were. I told him that the one glued to Cody's arm is his future wife and the other one is her sister. He wanted to know if either of you would like to go out on a date. I told him you were not allowed to go out with ghosts." We all laughed, then Grandpa explained to Pierre what was said and even he smiled.

Grandpa took the sword from Uncle Eric and Pierre picked up his sword from the ground; he and grandpa began to duel. You could tell that Pierre was really trying to get the better of Grandpa but Grandpa was way too quick for him. They had been fighting for what seemed like a long time when Pierre's big floppy hat with the long feather went flying from his head. He stepped back and tucked his sword under his arm; he and Grandpa had another talk, then he turned, walked over and picked up his hat and put it back on his head, turned again and faced Grandpa. He stood there like he was waiting for something. Grandpa put the sword back in its scabbard and the ghost vanished.

Grandpa explained that, "Pierre said I was just playing with him and he was tired of me knocking his hat off so he wasn't going to play anymore today. He wanted to go home." I was a little disappointed when I looked at my watch and discovered that the whole event had only lasted about twenty minutes. We all headed back to Uncle Eric's house to do some fencing, which was a good excuse for me to be hanging out with Maggie.

CHAPTER THREE: BOBBY

Early that morning, as Shelley and Maggie were getting ready to go out to watch the battle and be scared by the ghost, they were trying to be quiet but their older brother, Bobby, heard them and woke up. This guy was nineteen, and a real bum: pony tail, no job, a little guy with a big chip on his shoulder. Hearing all the subdued and excited chatter, he decided to go out on the deck with his binoculars and see if he could see what was going on. He saw his sisters on the path to Eric's house and watched them walking down through the woods with Eric, his son, his nephew, and some other dude. They stopped in some clearing but he couldn't see what they were doing from where he was. He walked down to the far end of the deck but he still couldn't see too well as there was too much brush in the way. He went back in the house, put on a jacket and boots, and went back out, down through the wood to a spot from which he could see into the clearing with his binoculars but not be seen by his prey.

"Wow, Eric and some little dude in a three musketeer outfit are sword fighting. Man, it looks like those are real swords and they are really trying to kill each other," he muttered to himself while he watched. He stayed hidden and watched the whole thing; he even saw the little guy disappear. He pulled the glasses away from his eyes, blinked, and looked again. The little guy was gone. Everyone was leaving the woods for Eric's house. Nobody acted like anything was wrong. Waiting until everyone had left, and whispering, "What's going on here?" he went down there to see what he could see. Nothing. No tracks leading away from where the little guy had been; in fact, no tracks at all. Nothing.

He went back home. He sat in his room talking to himself, but he couldn't figure it out. He had been staring right at the musketeer dude when he just vanished. He couldn't remember looking away, or even blinking, but it seemed that the guy didn't vanish; it was more like he faded away right before your eyes. Now he didn't know what to think. He didn't believe in ghosts. He could ask his sisters, but they didn't get along too well so they probably wouldn't tell him anything. He could ask Ryan. He was just a kid, and if he was sneaky enough, he was pretty sure he could worm it out of him. "Okay, that's the plan then."

Bobby decided to go over to Eric and Ryan's house to see what he could find out. He waited until he saw a yellow truck leave, then went down through the woods and in the back way to the house. Before he stepped out of the last screen of bushes, he stopped. He could hear swords clicking together, so he peeked through the shrubs to see what was going on. Ryan and his cousin Cody had on big gloves and fencing masks, and were working out with fencing swords. Maggie and Shelley were watching. After a few minutes, the boys stopped, took off the gloves and masks, and gave them to the girls. He thought, *This should be funny.* After watching them for a while, he decided, "Hey, they are not too bad. Not as good as the boys, but not bad." As he watched them practice he devised a plan. He guessed that if he came out of the woods everyone would leave, since nobody liked him; then he could corner Ryan by asking him to show him a few moves with the sword.

He stepped around the bushes like he had just walked down the path and acted surprised that the girls were fencing. He said, "Cool! So that's what you've been doing over here lately." The girls stopped, took off the gloves and masks, and handed all the gear to Cody to put away. They all started walking toward the house. Bobby yelled, "Hey, wait, Ryan. How about showing me some of those moves? You wouldn't want my sisters better at sword fighting than I am, would you?"

Cody stopped and looked at Ryan. Ryan squinted his eyes and nodded. "Oh, yeah, it would be really bad for a girl to be able to be better than you. Give me the stuff, Cody." Ryan and Bobby went out to the middle of the back yard and started the lesson. First Ryan showed Bobby how to stand, then the guard positions, then some of the moves. After some fifteen minutes they stopped for a break and Bobby said, "I watched your dad and that other guy sword fighting with the little three musketeers guy. They arc really good."

"Yeah, that other guy is my grandpa. He is the best of all of us with a sword. He and my dad took lessons,"

Ryan informed him.

"Yeah, those blades were flashing back and forth so fast I could hardly see them.

By the way, how does your grandpa make him disappear like that?"

"I don't know. When Grandpa or Dad is ready to fight, old Pierre appears and when they are ready to quit, he disappears."

"Is he a ghost?" Bobby asked himself, but he decided not to ask Ryan. He didn't want to make him clam up so he changed the subject. "Man, I would sure like to watch your Grandpa work with a sword again. When is he coming back?"

"In about a month," Ryan informed him. "I'll let you know, but you better stay out of sight when Grandpa and Dad are fighting Pierre. Grandpa is getting a little worried about all the people finding out about this. If he gets too worried, he won't come back."

"That would be too bad. That was really exciting. Have you or Cody had a chance to fight the ghost yet? Uh, what did you say his name was?".

"His name is Pierre, and no, Grandpa says we aren't good enough yet. Besides I'm not sure I want to. He is out to kill someone for some kind of vengeance, and I don't really want to be the one."

"I can understand that. Those swords look dangerous." After working for another fifteen minutes, Ryan put away the fencing gear, and Bobby went home.

He was pretty excited. He hadn't believed in ghosts, but there was no other explanation for what he had seen, and Ryan had confirmed it. Now he had to think of a way he could use this to make some money. Bobby went to his room, tripped over a pile of junk on his floor, skipped one-footed to his unmade bed and flopped down. He had to think. The first thought that came to his mind was blackmail. Eric lived in a big house, had a summer home down on the sound, drove a new, big pickup truck, and had a big boat on a trailer in his back yard so he must have money. The only trouble with the plan was that he would have to be real sneaky about it. If Eric discovered who was doing the blackmailing it would be the end of Bobby, and the thought of being beaten to death by a monster like Eric was not a pleasant thought. He considered the media. Maybe the tabloids would be willing to pay for a good ghost story. He decided he had to check it out. Yeah, man. If this worked out, he could be rich. He could get his own place; he could buy a new car instead of driving that old piece of junk his folks had bought him.

This could be great. Bobby jumped off his bed, almost tripping over the same pile of junk on his way to the door. He ran out to his car, and sped off to the store to buy the tabloids. He needed the phone numbers to get this started.

CHAPTER FOUR: CODY

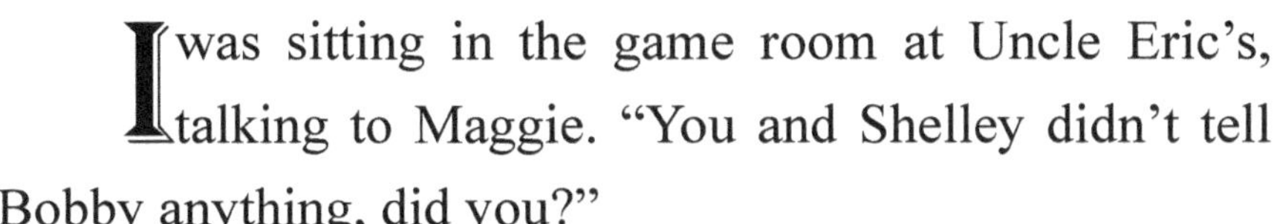

I was sitting in the game room at Uncle Eric's, talking to Maggie. "You and Shelley didn't tell Bobby anything, did you?"

"I know I didn't and I don't think Shelley did either but it is a bit strange that he showed up when he did. I had better keep an eye on him." But it was too late. A month later the weekend arrived that Grandpa was due to show up. We had been practicing as much as we could so we would be ready. Maggie said that she had been watching Bobby and that nothing out of the ordinary seemed to be going on. Grandpa and his yellow four-wheel drive truck rolled in on Friday night. He rolled down the window and called, "Hi Cody, how has your practicing been going since my last visit?"

"Great! I'm ready for the big time, Grandpa. Wait and see."

"Yeah, sure, Hot Shot. We'll see what Eric says."

Mom and my sister Mariah came out of the house and Grandpa had to do all that hugging and kissing stuff, ending our conversation. Later we all went over to Uncle Eric's house for dinner. I rode with Grandpa so we could talk some more, and I could try to convince him that I was ready to take on Pierre but he said, "Cody, you are my favorite grandson. I love you, and I don't want anything to happen to you. Pierre is not just fencing, he is trying to get revenge by killing someone, and I don't want it to be you. If something happened to you, your mother and my wife would take turns beating me to death with baseball bats."

"But, Grandpa, you and Eric do it, and I am dying to try."

"Yeah, dying just might be the right word there. Think about that. If that happened, your mom and grandmother would make sure that my funeral would closely follow yours. Besides, if Eric and I get carved up a little, everyone would say it was our own fault for taking the chance. If you got hurt I would get the blame."

"You said you would talk to Eric and see what he says. Okay?"

"Okay, but all you want to do is impress that red head and she is already mad about you so why take the chance?" Grandpa laughed and I blushed and that was the end of that until we got to Uncle Eric's house.

After dinner, Grandpa, Uncle Eric, Ryan and I went into the garage and got out the fencing gear so I could show Grandpa how great I was. It was dark outside, so we worked out in the garage. Grandpa and Uncle Eric went first ,and then I practiced with Uncle Eric. After a few minutes, Grandpa took the sword from Uncle Eric, and said, "Okay, Cody, let me see how good you are."

Grandpa would never be called a good fencer. He doesn't advance and retreat. He just stands in one spot and makes you do all the footwork. He doesn't wear a mask and doesn't worry about it because nobody can touch him with their sword. He's too fast. If you thrust or slash or chop at him, his sword is always there to meet yours; when his sword has stopped your move it will come flicking back at you so quick you can hardly see it so you don't want to get too close. I did my best for about five minutes. My sword arm was getting tired. Grandpa stepped back, dropped his sword tip and said, "Not bad. What do you think, Eric?"

"I think he is about as good as me."

"He wants to fight Pierre to impress the red head." Everyone laughed it up, except me. Uncle Eric studied me for a while. "I don't know if you are that good, Cody. That old ghost is dangerous. We will work out really hard this next month and, if you can beat me, then maybe. Is that okay with you, Pop?" Grandpa stared at me for a few seconds. "Well, maybe." We put the fencing stuff away then and went in the house. Dawn would come early and so would Pierre.

CHAPTER FIVE: BOBBY

Bobby had been real busy that month, too. He had to wait each day for his family to leave the house before he could do anything. After his sisters left for school he would go to work. He called all the tabloids but no one would believe his ghost story. He finally talked one of them into sending out a reporter to talk to him. He asked the guy to meet him at a restaurant in the city. The guy was on time. He had described himself on the phone so Bobby recognized him when he walked into the place. He walked over to the guy's table, and said, "Hi, I'm Bobby." The guy stood up. He was close to six feet tall and fat.

"Hi, I'm Tom Carson." They sat down; when the waitress came they ordered pie and coffee. While they were eating, Bobby told Mr. Carson the whole story as he understood it. Mr. Carson thought about it while he ate. Eating seemed to be his number one priority in life. When he had finished his pie, he sat back, took a sip of his coffee, and said, "That's a pretty wild story, kid. Can we get pictures and maybe even some sound track?"

"No problem. We would have to do it from about a hundred yards away with long range stuff, maybe from a blind in the trees. If they figure out that we are up to something, the old man won't bring the ghost out and we won't get anything."

"You mean this old man you talk about has some kind of control over the ghost?"

"Yes. I haven't figured out yet how he does it but when they are ready he makes it appear and, when they want to quit, he makes it disappear."

Tom Carson had been in tabloid journalism for ten years and wasn't easily fooled by scam artists. He had a feeling the kid was for real. "Okay, give me your number. I'll talk it over with my editor. If he likes it, I'll get back to you in a few days."

Bobby could see money coming his way. "Great! Here is my number. I wrote it on this paper for you. You know we have to keep this quiet until we get the pictures and stuff, right?"

"I'll be very discreet, Bobby, I promise." The fat man dumped some money on the table to pay the bill.

On the way back to his office at the paper, Mr. Carson thought about what Bobby had told him. If all of it was true, it would make a good story but he would really like to know the whole story. The grandfather was probably the only one who could tell it all the way through. That could wait. First he had to substantiate the thing with some pictures. He also had a feeling Bobby was going to want some money so he was going to have to go over the whole thing with his boss and decide on how much they were willing to pay the kid.

Mr. Carson went in the side door that is close to the parking area. As he went by security the guard stopped him. "Mr. Kowoski wants to see you right away." Tom mumbled something in response, went down the hall and took the elevator to the third floor office of the editor of the rag sheet he worked for. He stopped at the desk of the bosses' secretary. "Hello, beautiful. I hear the boss wants to see me."

The very pretty, very shapely, very blond young lady smiled up at him. "He saw you drive in. He's waiting for you. Go on in."

"He walked past the beauty queen, and through the door into the big office. The boss, a short, bald, overweight guy of about fifty, looked up from some copy he was reading. "Where you been? What's happening with that story about the senator that you were working on? We need something good for this issue, and all I got so far is junk."

While the boss was talking, Tom pulled out a chair and sat down. When the boss was finished, he said, "The story on the senator is coming along fine. I will have it for you in two more days but I think I have something for you for next month that you are going to like." He went through the story as Bobby told it and then went into what he thought of Bobby.

Mr. Kowoski agreed that the story sounded pretty good, and that Bobby would probably want a lot of money. "Okay. Keep on it. Offer him ten grand and let him work you up to twenty five or thirty, but don't go over fifty. If you do, I'll take it out of your pay." The last part of that was loud enough for the secretary outside to hear.

Bobby was getting nervous. He had been able to

get a blind set up during the day. It was far enough away from any houses that nobody could see what they were doing and the crew was quiet so no one came around to investigate. The negotiations on the money had gone pretty well even though it wasn't exactly what he had wanted. He would end up with fifty thousand if all went well. He had already received ten grand. He would get another fifteen when they saw the ghost and the rest if the pictures came out.

Everything was ready except for the cameras. They would be brought in before daylight on the day of the battle. The long range listening device would come with the rest of the equipment. Bobby was proud of himself because, in the negotiations for the money, he would not even tell them where he lived until he got the ten grand and had their promise for the rest of the money in writing.

The waiting was killing him. He had been bugging Ryan but each time he asked Ryan would just say that he hadn't heard yet. Having to go over there and act all buddy-buddy with a twelve-year-old kid was a real drag. He hated fencing with him but the worst part was that he couldn't beat him. The one time Bobby challenged Cody to a fight was a big mistake. Maggie and Shelley got a big kick out of that. *"Well, laugh it up*," he thought. *"I'm the one who will end up with the dough.*"

Bobby could always tell when Cody was over at Ryan's house, because his sisters would go over. He was pretty sure one of them was in love. When the girls went over there on Wednesday after school, he waited for a while, until he thought most of the fencing would be over and then ambled over. When he arrived, Cody and Ryan were still practicing; Eric was coaching. Bobby sat down in a lawn chair by Shelley to watch. When the boys quit, it was the girl's turn. Eric usually went in the house about this time, but today he stayed and watched while Cody coached. When Shelley and Maggie stopped for a break, Eric said, "You girls are doing well. Dad will be here this weekend so come over after school Friday to show him what you can do. He'll be impressed."

Bobby had a hard time keeping himself from jumping up and running for home. Although the girl's excitement was enough to provide cover for him, he forced himself to sit still and wait. After Eric went into the house and the girls quit celebrating and went back to practicing, Bobby slipped away and ran for home. He ran into the house and up to his room to get Tom Carson's card and call him. Tom answered on the second ring.

"Hey, Tom, this is Bobby. I just got the word. It's

this Saturday."

"Okay, Bobby, we will be there about an hour and a half before dawn. That way no one will see us. Just make sure you don't wake anybody up, and mess it up."

"Yeah, I'll be careful. I'll see you then."

Bobby had that stuff all figured out. He planned to sleep out under the back deck in his sleeping bag with a tarp over him. That way no one would hear the alarm on his cell phone go off that early in the morning. When his alarm went off at 4:00 a.m. he crawled out from under the deck. The night was very dark with clouds obscuring the stars and moon. There was a street light in front of the house, but it didn't light up much of the woods and brush. He didn't know how the camera crew would make it to the blind in the dark. He had a flash light but he was afraid to use it. What if someone saw it and called the cops? Even though it wasn't illegal to be there, an investigating officer would mess everything up.

He felt his way through the brush. When he banged into a tree he gave up. Holding his fingers over the lens so just a little light came out, he turned on the flash light. When he got to the blind, he found the camera and sound guys already there. They were too busy setting up to pay him any attention. There was not enough room in the blind for him so, after climbing up and looking around from the ladder, he climbed back down. He was a little upset about not being able to watch from the blind but thought he had better go back to the spot he had watched from the first time he spied on the ghost.

He was about to leave when he heard someone coming. He couldn't see a light or anything, but there was definitely someone moving toward him. He froze. Then out of the dark he heard Tom Carson's voice.

"Good morning, Bobby," he said, just above a whisper.

"It's darker than ten feet down. How did you see to get through the woods?"

"Night vision glasses. How are things going up there?"

"I think they are about ready. There is not enough room for me, but I have a good place to watch from if you have binoculars."

"I'll kick the sound man out. I want to see what the cameras see. Why don't you wait for him? He will probably want to see the fight, too."

While Bobby waited, Tom climbed up to the blind and a few minutes later the sound man came down.

"Too bad we can't watch from up there," Bobby

complained.

"No, the platform will barely hold the fat man. It would come crashing down if all of us tried to stay up there."

The sky was starting to get light enough to see a little, so they took off for Bobby's viewing spot. After they had settled in to wait, Bobby, in whispers, introduced himself to the sound man who in tum said, "My name is Willie. How long before they show up?" Bobby heard a door slam shut at his house and responded, "In just a few minutes. There go my sisters now."

CHAPTER SIX: CODY

Maggie and Shelley took so long getting ready that they were a few minutes late. We took our regular places around the clearing. After Grandpa checked all around for spies, we were ready. Eric pulled the haunted sword from its scabbard and we waited. Usually it only took a few seconds but today it was a couple of minutes before we heard the wind and the rattle of armor. Maggie put an iron grip on my arm when Pierre strolled into view. Instead of going right into the guard position as he usually did, he walked over to Grandpa and began to converse in French.

"Good morning, my friend. The last time we met you knocked my hat off, so I would rather fight you today, if you don't mind." Grandpa translated. He turned to Uncle Eric and took the sword. Before they started, Pierre again said something in French to which Grandpa responded, "Ryan, run up to my truck and get my cowboy hat for me. Pierre says it's not fair that I don't have a hat to knock off." We all laughed and Ryan took off for the house.

Grandpa and Pierre stood talking in French until Ryan came back. Grandpa put his hat on and pulled it down tight so it wouldn't fall off easily then Grandpa and Pierre went to work. That was some battle. Pierre was trying real hard to get at Grandpa's hat, and Grandpa was working to make sure he didn't. Normally they would fight for about five minutes and take a break, but today they went for more than ten minutes before Pierre stepped back and lowered his blade. They talked for a few minutes more in French.

Grandpa started to turn to say something to Eric when Pierre lunged but he wasn't fast enough. Grandpa's sword came up and around with the speed of light and hit Pierre's sword a tremendous blow right at the hilt. It sent the sword spinning from his hand; it flew about a dozen feet before landing in the soggy leaves. Pierre stared at Grandpa for a few seconds then turned and walked over to pick up his sword. Grandpa followed; he waited until Pierre had picked up his sword and was ready, then reached out with his sword and knocked Pierre's hat off. Pierre stared at Grandpa for a long fifteen seconds, reached down, picked up his hat, put it on, and attacked.

This time there was no fooling around. They were both angry. They slashed and stabbed at each other for five full minutes. It ended when Pierre made a wild swing at Grandpa's head. Grandpa blocked it and then he slashed Pierre from his right shoulder to his belly button. Pierre dropped his sword and stepped back; they just stared at each other. Pierre's clothes and skin were laid wide open, but no blood came out. It was real creepy and Maggie had that grip on my arm again. Shelley started babbling, "Oh my god! He is slashed open and there isn't any blood." Uncle Eric commanded, "Shut up, Shelley."

Grandpa said something to Pierre in French and Pierre answered him. Eric handed the sheath to Grandpa and he put the sword away. Pierre, holding himself together with his left hand, bent down, picked up his sword and faded away. I was feeling a little sick, not because the ghost got cut but because if I had been fighting Pierre today, it probably would have been me and not Pierre that ended up all cut up, and I do bleed.

We were all a little solemn as we walked back to Uncle Eric's house that day. No one said anything. We were all wondering what would happen to Pierre and whether, when we pulled out the haunted sword the next time, he would appear still wounded or would he be all fixed up or would he appear at all.

Uncle Eric asked Grandpa what that last conversation was all about. "I told him I was sorry and asked him if he would he like to go home. He said yes."

CHAPTER SEVEN: BOBBY

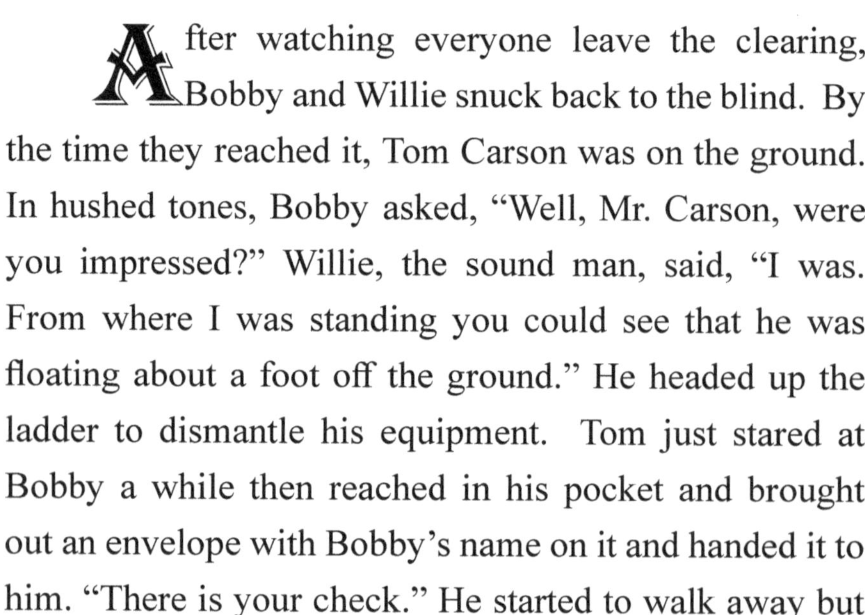

After watching everyone leave the clearing, Bobby and Willie snuck back to the blind. By the time they reached it, Tom Carson was on the ground. In hushed tones, Bobby asked, "Well, Mr. Carson, were you impressed?" Willie, the sound man, said, "I was. From where I was standing you could see that he was floating about a foot off the ground." He headed up the ladder to dismantle his equipment. Tom just stared at Bobby a while then reached in his pocket and brought out an envelope with Bobby's name on it and handed it to him. "There is your check." He started to walk away but turned back to stare at Bobby. "He was slashed wide open and not a drop of blood. He just faded away. You'll get the rest of the money if the pictures come out."

Bobby was not worried about that. He had twenty five grand and was so excited that he almost wet his pants. Tom had told him when he gave him the first check to rent a post office box and open a new account at a different bank with the box as the address. If his folks would happen to see his bank statement and open it, there would be questions about the source of all that money. Bobby was instructed to remember not to throw a lot of money around until after the article was printed; after that it didn't matter. Bobby was headed for town but first he had to stop at the house to pee.

Tom Carson walked right past Kowoski's secretary and into the boss's office. When the floor started shaking, Mr. Kowoski knew it was either an earthquake or Tom Carson was entering his office in a hurry. He didn't look up from his work. "Okay. I hope you are going to tell me all went well and we have a great story. I don't want to hear that the blind fell down under that great weight."

"I dropped off the film at the developer for the still shots. One of the video cameras only showed a misty cloud for the ghost. The other one has a fairly clear picture." He went over to the VCR and put in the cassette. Kowoski picked up the remote and turned everything on. He watched the whole thing, then ran it back and watched it again. He sat for a minute thinking about what he had seen. His first question was, "No blood?"

"Yes, that was a little shocking to me, too. I guess that's about what you'd expect though, under the circumstances, given that he is a ghost."

"The sound was good, too. We need to get the French translated, though. How hard is it going to be to get the whole story?"

"I don't know, but I think I'd like to shoot it again the next time they fight."

"Yes, I am dying to see if the wounded ghost can make it back. It will be interesting to see what condition he's in. Do they do ghostly stitches in his hide and provide a new shirt from his wardrobe back in Spookville?"

Tom got through to Bobby that night. Shelley answered the phone. Tom asked for Bobby. "Is he there?"

"Yes, may I ask who is calling?"

"This is Tom. I'm a friend of his"

"Okay. I'll call him. Bobby, phone," she yelled

up the stairs. She listened until Bobby picked up the phone and then hung up.

When Bobby answered with a surly, "Yeah?" Tom said, "We need to talk. I'll meet you at the restaurant at nine tomorrow morning."

"What's up?"

"I'll tell you then. See you tomorrow."

This time Bobby was there first. When Tom arrived Bobby was eating an omelet. He had a piece of pie sitting there for Tom, who eased himself into his chair and proceeded to devour it. The waitress brought him coffee and some more hot chocolate for Bobby.

After Tom finished his pie, he told Bobby, "Some of the pictures came out, enough to give you the rest of the money. The boss would like something more for his money though." Bobby started to get mad, but Tom cut him off with a wave of his hand. "It's just a little thing; he wants you to tell us when the next fight is. We want to see if the ghost comes back and if he is stitched up or healed up or what. This is a good story, Bobby. We want to see more."

"Are you going to hold the rest of my money 'til then?"

"No, it's here in my pocket, but how about it?"

"Okay, but I'll want another two thousand."

Bobby paid the check. As they left the restaurant Tom gave him another envelope. Bobby headed for the bank and Tom left for his office. He had other stories to work on, but this one was turning out to be a great one.

CHAPTER EIGHT: CODY

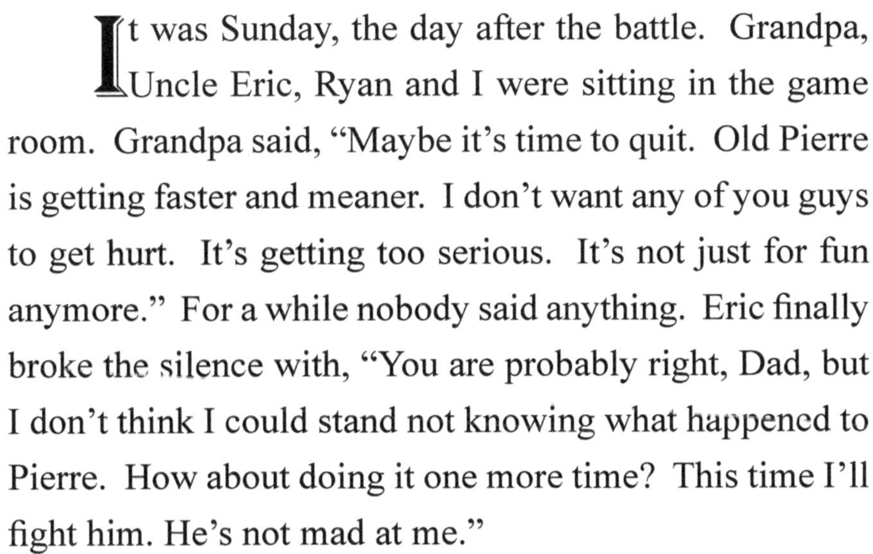

It was Sunday, the day after the battle. Grandpa, Uncle Eric, Ryan and I were sitting in the game room. Grandpa said, "Maybe it's time to quit. Old Pierre is getting faster and meaner. I don't want any of you guys to get hurt. It's getting too serious. It's not just for fun anymore." For a while nobody said anything. Eric finally broke the silence with, "You are probably right, Dad, but I don't think I could stand not knowing what happened to Pierre. How about doing it one more time? This time I'll fight him. He's not mad at me."

"All right, let's make it next weekend. I'm worried

about Pierre, too."

"Why so soon?"

"I have a fishing trip in Canada planned for the next two weeks." Ryan and I yelled at him for not taking us, but school was still on and we knew we wouldn't be allowed to miss it. He said he would take us during the summer for a couple of weeks so we let him off the hook.

My mom came to pick me up about the time grandpa was ready to leave. While everyone was out in the driveway saying goodbye, Ryan sneaked off to Bobby's house. Bobby's mom answered the door. When he asked if he could see Bobby, she said, "Come on in, Ryan. As you can tell, he is up in his room. That music is loud enough to rattle the windows. Go on up, knock loud or he won't hear you."

Bobby looked angry when he answered the door, but when he saw it was Ryan he motioned him in, shut the door, and went over to turn his music down.

"Did you get to see it this time?"

"Yeah, your grandpa sliced him wide open. I suppose that will be the last of that."

"No, they want to see what happens to Pierre, so they are going to do it again next weekend."

CHAPTER NINE: BOBBY

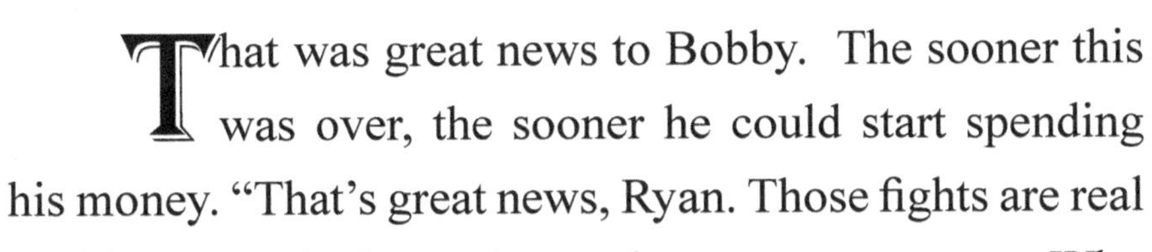

That was great news to Bobby. The sooner this was over, the sooner he could start spending his money. "That's great news, Ryan. Those fights are real exciting. Look, I was just going to go to town. Why don't you come over tomorrow night? You know, so we can hang out and talk about it."

As soon as Bobby got rid of Ryan, he changed clothes and called Tom on his cell phone and asked him to meet him at the restaurant. When Tom got there Bobby was eating dinner. Tom sat down and said, "Okay. I'm here. What's the big deal now?" Around a mouthful of food,

Bobby said, "They are going to do it again next weekend. They are worried about their ghost." The waitress came over; Tom ordered pie and coffee. This was good news to him, too. It meant he could get his story in an earlier edition, which would make his boss happy.

"Good. We will need to be ready by the same time Saturday morning, right?"

"I think so. If l hear any different I'll let you know." Tom would be glad to be done with this one so he didn't have to deal with this creep anymore.

CHAPTER TEN: CODY

Friday came and grandpa got to my house just as I got home from school.

He climbed out of that bright yellow truck and yelled at me as I was coming down the street, "Hey, Cody, how goes the war?" I ran up to him, gave him a hug, "Things are happening, Grandpa. How are you doing?"

"I'm doing pretty well for an old guy."

Then mom and my sister came out, and there were lots of hugs and stuff going on for a while. Grandpa and I finally got out of there and headed for Uncle Eric's house in grandpa's yellow four wheel drive pickup. For a guy on social security, he's pretty hip. On the way, we talked about school, fighting Pierre, and Maggie and me. He was a little worried about my grades with all my extra activities. I told him I was doing fine. He said he would check on it with my mom; I wasn't worried.

When we got to Uncle Eric's house, grandpa grabbed his bag and went in. I had more important things to do. I headed through the woods to Maggie's house. Shelley answered the door, said, "Hi Cody," then turned and yelled, "Cody's here." Maggie came from the kitchen wearing an apron. She looked great. She gave me a little kiss, said "Hi, Cody," took my hand and led me into the kitchen. "I'm fixing dinner. Hamburger Helper. What are you up to?"

"We are practicing hard tonight. We're fighting tomorrow." She gave me a worried look, "So soon?"

"Yeah, Uncle Eric and grandpa are worried about Pierre."

"Aren't you worried, too?"

"No, he is a ghost. I'm more worried about Uncle Eric and grandpa. They can get hurt." I don't know why I said that. I guess it had been on my mind.

"Yes, after that sneaky trick Pierre tried to pull last week, I'm worried, too. If your grandpa wasn't so quick he might have been killed."

"Thank you for worrying about grandpa. He does take too many chances."

The next morning everybody and everything was in place by daylight. Bobby and the sound man, Willie, were in their hiding place. Tom and the camera man were in the blind with the equipment. We were arranged around the clearing ready to go. There was one addition to the watchers. Mr. Kowoski was sitting on a rung of the ladder to the blind with binoculars around his neck.

It was decided that since Pierre was not mad at Uncle Eric he would do the dueling today. Eric looked around, took a deep breath, and drew the sword. Today there was no waiting. The wind blew, the armor rattled, Maggie gripped my arm, and Pierre appeared. He looked the same as the last time we saw him. His clothes and chest were still slashed wide open. He walked to the center of the clearing, turned to grandpa, said something in French, turned back to Uncle Eric and attacked.

Uncle Eric is a big man and strong, but today it took all of his strength to counter old Pierre's attack. The fight was furious. After seven or eight minutes,

Pierre stepped back and lowered his sword; Eric saluted with his. When his sword reached the end of its sweep, it happened. Pierre lunged. Eric saw it coming too late. He turned and swung his sword back to block it, but about three inches of Pierre's blade went into Eric's shoulder muscle.

I shook loose from Maggie's arm and charged. So did grandpa. Uncle Eric stepped back, swung his sword over and down hard enough to knock Pierre's sword into the dirt at his feet. I got there in time to stomp on Pierre's sword before he could pick it up and do more damage. I looked to see how Uncle Eric was doing. Grandpa took a hankie from his pocket and stuffed it inside Uncle Eric's shirt over the wound to stop the bleeding. Maggie screamed, "Look out, Cody." I looked just in time to see Pierre snatch his sword out from under my foot and lunge at Grandpa's back. I lunged too. I hit him in the sword arm, but he still managed to get the blade a few inches into grandpa.

When he saw grandpa stagger into Eric, Mr. Kowoski yanked out his cell phone and dialed 911. While I wrestled with Pierre, Ryan grabbed the sword from Uncle Eric and, picking up the scabbard, put the sword away. Pierre started to fade out of my grasp. Uncle Eric was holding grandpa up, asking him, "Dad, are you still with us?" Grandpa just growled which made me feel better; if he could growl, he wasn't too bad off.

Just about then Bobby and Willie showed up. Shelly said, "What are you doing here, Bobby? Who's this guy?"

"We were watching. Is he dead?" Tom came wheezing up with Mr. Kowoski right behind him. Uncle Eric, supporting grandpa with Willie's help, started moving toward the house. Mr. Kowoski turned to Tom, "I called for an ambulance. Go up to the road and direct them to the right place." Tom grabbed Bobby and ordered him to go up to the road and see to it that the medics get to the right house. All of us, by then, were on the trail to Eric's house. I was mumbling a little prayer for grandpa when I realized Maggie was stuck to my arm again. She looked at me with tears in her eyes, "Your poor grandpa. Will he be all right?"

Something else came to mind then. "Not when Shannon gets ahold of him." Someone was going to have to call her. She is his wife. Oh boy, after fooling her with that video of us throwing the sword in the sound, it is not going to be safe around here for any of us. Oh, yeah, and what about my Mom? She loves her daddy very much. She is going to have a very large piece of my hide, too. I hope I have enough to go around.

They got grandpa into the game room, which was the room closest to the back yard. I threw the cushions from the couch on the floor so we could lay him down on his face to look at his wound. Aunt Andrea came in, took a look around, and shrieked, "Oh my god! What happened to you two?"

"It's a long story. Call an ambulance." Grandpa turned to Tom and Mr. Kowoski and demanded, "What's your story?"

Tom wheezed, "We already called the medics; they are on the way."

Mr. Kowoski began to explain, "We are from a local magazine. We heard about you sword fighting with a ghost and came to see for ourselves. You may end up being glad we were here. We filmed the whole thing. When he gets to a hospital and they see that it's a stab wound, they are going to call the cops."

He was right. We followed the ambulance to the hospital in Uncle Eric's van. We left Ryan home to explain everything to his mom. I was hoping someone else would call Shannon. While they were working on grandpa, a nurse cleaned up Uncle Eric's shoulder and bandaged it. When the cops showed up, Uncle Eric told me to call Shannon while he talked to them. I knew I was going to get stuck with calling her. I just knew it. He told me to tell her that it was a little accident and to fly over here so she could drive him home in his truck. I took his cell phone and dialed the number.

I call Shannon Nana because she is grandpa's second wife and not my real grandma. I love her anyway. Her son Rick answered the phone. "Hello."

"Hello, Rick, this is Cody. Can I talk to Nana?" He laid the phone down. Pretty soon she picked it up and said, "Hi, Cody. How are you, honey?" I was worried; I had to do this just right or I was in big trouble with everyone.

"I am doing well, Nana, but grandpa had a little accident and would like you to fly over here so you can drive him home in his truck."

"What kind of accident, Cody? Is he hurt bad?"

"No, but he said if you don't fly over here to get him, he will stay here until he feels good enough to drive himself home."

"Okay, Cody, but I would still like to know what kind of accident he had."

"Oh, we were messing around in the woods and I was trying to hit him and he stepped backwards and fell over a rock and landed on a log with a sharp broken limb sticking up. It jabbed him in the back but he's not hurt bad; it's up by his shoulder and not too deep." By then I was sweating like a fountain. Uncle Eric and the cops had been listening to my end of the conversation. Uncle Eric took the phone and told Nana that grandpa was in the clinic getting it cleaned up and, if she didn't feel like coming over, that Pop could stay at his place for a few days until he felt like going home. Then he told her that he would pay the bill at the clinic, not to worry. He said he would have grandpa call her when they were through with him. He turned to us and said, "She is not going to fly over here until she talks to dad."

The police officer asked, "Did you and your dad trip over the same rock and fall on the same sharp stick?"

"How did you know?"

"Oh, it was just a guess. I think I'll wait around and talk to your dad just to see if he agrees with your story."

Before Grandpa was done getting patched up, Tom Carson showed up and handed his card to the officer. He said, "We were filming the action today when these two guys received their wounds, so if you would like to see it all on tape just stop by the office any time." The officer knew Tom and the rag he worked for; they talked for a few minutes and they walked out together. About twenty minutes later, the doctor came out.

"Well, it's not too bad. The blade slid between the ribs, but at an angle from down at say waist high, going up so it missed the lung but did get into the lung cavity. We are going to have to keep him for a few days to make sure it's draining properly and that there is no fluid build-up." Uncle Eric thanked him and asked if we could see him.

"Yes, but he needs rest so don't talk too long."

Uncle Eric, Maggie, and I all trouped into Grandpa's room. He was just lying there with a hose coming out of his back. Uncle Eric leaned over and in a soft voice asked, "Are you awake, Dad?" Grandpa didn't open his eyes but he answered, "No. Do I look awake?" Uncle Eric smiled a little; he knew if the old man was making jokes he wasn't dead yet.

"I called Shannon. Or Cody did. Anyway, Cody made up this wild tale about you falling back on log with a sharp broken off branch that stuck you. I told her you weren't hurt too bad. I told her that she didn't need to fly over here, that in a few days you could drive yourself home. She said she would decide that after she had talked to you. Are you up to that now?" Grandpa opened his eyes, looked at Eric, and said, "You had better dial her up." Eric dialed the number, and when Nana answered he said, "Hi, Shannon. Here he is." He handed the phone to Grandpa.

He listened to her for a few seconds, then said, "Yes, that's about the way it happened. Cody was a little excited, so his version probably sounded pretty bad. I don't know. I didn't hear it." He listened for a while then said, "I'll be home in four or five days. And I love you too." He handed the phone to Uncle Eric, "Cody, you had better call your mom and tell her your big story if she hasn't already heard it from Aunt Andrea. Eric, call Andrea and tell her what to say if Shannon calls. Now get out of here and let a man rest."

We left. We were walking down the hall toward the front desk when around the corner came Mom. She stopped in front of us, looked up at her brother Eric and said, "So you didn't throw the sword away. Well, you had better start playing up being wounded to keep from getting beat half to death." Uncle Eric is a foot taller than his sister and a hundred pounds heavier but he always backs down when she's mad at him.

"Okay. Okay. I screwed up, but don't go in there and yell at Pop. He doesn't need that right now. He'll be all right in a few days; then you can beat him up."

She just glared at him for a second then turned to me, "You are in big trouble, young man."

"Yes, ma'am."

Maggie spoke up then. "Now, listen, this was not Cody's doing. If he hadn't jumped in and fought with Pierre your dad would probably be dead right now." You had to be proud of that redhead's fire. She stood right up to them.

Uncle Eric chimed in, "She is right. Cody saved us for sure. And Maggie is right about the blame being all on me, too. Dad didn't even know about me keeping the sword and faking the video that we sent to Shannon. Now have Cody tell you the story that we made up for Shannon so that she doesn't kill Dad herself."

Mom went in to see grandpa. She wasn't in there long, though. When she came out of the room she said, "I was trying to be nice, but he said he was tired, and for me to beat it." So we sat around and waited. A nurse came along later and said to go home. They would call us if anything happened.

A detective went with the cop to the magazine office to see the video of the fight. As soon as they got into Mr. Kowoski's office they started asking questions but

Mr. Kowoski told them, "I think it would be a lot better if you saw the film first and then asked your questions." After they watched both videos, the detective asked to see the second one again. "This looks like something straight out of Hollywood. This looks like one of your phony rag sheet stories. Even if this is true, nobody down at Headquarters is going to believe it."

"They will have to believe when they see it printed in our magazine."

The cop laughed. "They are sure not to believe it if you print it."

Mr. Kowoski turned red and started to say something back but the detective cut him off. "I guess we are going to have to put in the report the crazy story about him falling on a sharp stick. That's more believable than a ghost story. Anyway, nobody is making any charges. All we have to do is cover the doctor's report. Let's get out of here."

Mr. Kowoski protested, "We have a dozen witnesses to back up our story and besides, we haven't had time to doctor the films."

"You know, I might even believe it myself," the detective said, "after watching the films, but I'm pretty sure the chief won't. The sharp stick story is the one we are sticking with. Besides, you only want us to go along with your story to make it more believable. Sorry, you're on your own."

It was a week before grandpa was out of the hospital. On the day Uncle Eric brought him to his house we were all there and everything was ready. We had dug a hole at the back of Uncle Eric's property. He had bought a gun safe; it was sitting next to the hole, open and ready. Grandpa looked pretty good when he got out of the van and walked down to the burial spot. The whole family was there as well as Maggie and Shelley. Not Nana, though. We were still keeping her in the dark. Grandpa inspected the sword to make sure it was the right one this time. He handed it to Uncle Eric who put it in the safe and locked it. He handed the keys to my mom. It had been decided-- by her--that she was the one to dispose of them. Ryan and I lowered the safe into the hole. Uncle Eric, Ryan and I each took a shovel; in a few minutes the hole was filled in.

Grandpa said, "Well, it was fun while it lasted."

Mom muttered, "Like a bunch of little boys."

Aunt Andrea added, "Such foolishness. You could have all been killed."

Uncle Eric and grandpa looked a little sheepish, but I felt kind of proud of my part in it. We all went up to the house for dinner. Grandpa said he was leaving for home the next day. And that is pretty much the end of the story, except that when I was helping grandpa pack his bag, he said, "Here, put this in there," and he handed me a small key.

THE END

SMITTY'S RESCUE

CHAPTER ONE

His name is Wayne Smith but everyone calls him Smitty. He's a big guy, six one, broad and thick above the belt. Slender muscle and bone below . He doesn't have that Hollywood hero look, though. He has a large round face and thin hair. Not ugly but not handsome either, sort of the John Wayne look. Smitty grew up on a farm in the northwest and you could tell by his physique that he probably pulled the plow, the hay wagon, and the manure spreader, too. Everyone who knew him would tell you he was the nicest guy they knew; he was intelligent, too. He had a high I.Q., not quite genius but almost. So what's a guy like that doing in the Marines? In the Marine Boot Camp they tell you that the average I.Q. in the country is ninety-six, and that the average for the Marines is seventy-six. That's probably not true today since they quit taking prison sweepings and high school drop outs. Smitty didn't fit into any of those categories. He had a high school diploma, a year of college and was now a Corporal in charge of the radio operators in a mortar outfit with the Third Infantry Battalion. They had been in Nam for almost a year and had seen lots of action. Today they were flown over the lush jungle into this area by choppers. They had been there an hour and had all moved into their assigned positions. The infantry had moved out to set up the perimeter. Smitty and his buddy The Brick were digging a fox hole big enough for both of them and for their equipment to get out of the line of fire since radios had a bad habit of quitting when they were all shot up. When they finished digging their home away from home, Smitty asked, "Brick, our tour is going to be up in twenty three days, ten hours, and ten minutes. What are you going to do when you get home?"

"I've been sending half my pay home all thetime we've been over here. When I get home, I want to buy a nice car. I saved my money before we came over and when we stopped in Hong Kong I bought a couple tailor made suits. My folks live in a college town, and when I go home on leave I will look good driving around in my new car and clothes."

The talk went on as it always does when you're sitting in a fox hole waiting for someone to shoot at you. It was hot and muggy but they had dug their hole where it was partly in the shade so the afternoon sun wasn't beating right down into it. They were surprised that they had not met any resistance when they landed; however the two men had not been enjoying their leisure very long when a fire fight broke out on two sides of the field. The radio came to life with the F. O., or forward observer, asking for mortar rounds to be fired at the enemy out in front of them. The fire mission was relayed to the gunners and the guns started their whump whump whump noise. Smitty and The Brick went back to their conversation. The Brick remarked that, "It took those guys long enough to find us; we have been here almost two hours." Smitty sat up straight enough to see over the edge of the fox hole. "Yeah, the brass usually sets us down right in the middle of them. They must have missed by a couple of clicks this time. Hey, listen to that." Our mortars had finished their fire mission and stopped firing, but you could hear mortar shells that must be theirs still going off. The Brick was the radio operator here and had to stay with the mortars, but Smitty was the Corporal in charge of the communication squad and could move around. He waited until the shelling stopped, then grabbed his rifle and a hand held radio. "I'm going up there and take a look. I'll call you when I get some news." He started climbing out of the fox hole. The Brick grabbed him, and drug him back. About three months earlier Smitty's mortar squad and the platoon they were with ran into a large group of Viet Cong. Smitty carried five wounded men to the choppers, getting two minor wounds in the process.

"You already have a bunch of metals for carrying wounded back from a fire fight. You stay with the radio and I'll go."

"I have room on my chest for a few more metals. The F.O. and his radio man are my men. I have to see if I need to get replacements for them." Then he crawled over the edge and took off.

As he ran into the edge of the jungle, over the sound of the firing and the bullets zipping by, he could hear the screaming and moaning of the wounded. Just as he came up to the front lines, the mortar shells started coming in again. He had almost made it to the line of fox holes when something smacked him in the upper part of his left leg and he went down. Smitty knew he was hurt. He grabbed his rifle, checked to see that he still had his radio, and started crawling for the nearest fox hole. Through the smoke and dust from the shells going off, he could just make out two marines firing their rifles at ghostly figures out there in the gloom. Just as he was sliding head first over the back edge of the hole a shell went off right behind him, sending him flying the rest of the way into the fox hole and landing in a heap up against the legs of the two marines. One of the marines picked up Smitty's radio and called, "Hello, is anybody here?" The Brick answered, "Yeah, who wants to know?" The Marine keyed the radio again. "The guy who was carrying this radio is all tore up and there are a lot of other wounded up here, too. How about getting some medics moving our way? Over."

"They are on their way. Is my buddy dead?" The Marine answered, "No, but one foot is gone and the other leg has a hole in it."

The corpsmen had to wait for the shelling to stop before they could get to the front lines. The two guys in the fox hole lifted Smitty up onto the back edge of the hole and used his belt for a tourniquet on the leg with the missing foot. When the corpsmen got to Smitty they loaded him on a stretcher, patched up his other leg, and one of them asked, "What did you put him up here for? He could have been hit again." One of the guys in the fox hole answered, "He was leaking all over our house, and we are not due to clean it till Saturday."

"Marines! You jarheads are a cold hearted bunch." As the corpsmen moved off, one marine turned to the other and yelled over the noise of the fighting, "That pill pusher must be a new guy." The corpsmen with the Marines are Navy.

CHAPTER TWO

Smitty had been asleep a long time. The exploding shell that took his foot off and knocked him into the fox hole also knocked him out. He was unconscious during the entire time he was being carried to the choppers and flown to the hospital. He was starting to come out of the quiet fog; he sort of remembered the long sleep. It was the longest, quietest, coolest sleep he had had since coming to Nam. He kept his eyes closed, thinking, "There are no exploding shells, no gunfire, and it's not all hot and muggy. Maybe I'm in heaven. No, my left leg hurts, my right foot itches, and I'm dying of thirst." He opened his eyes and looked around. "Wow, everything is white and cool, and clean. Must be a hospital. Yeah, that's it. I was hit in the leg and they brought me here but I don't remember how I got here."

He was still wondering about that, when a nurse walked in. "Well, you're awake. I thought you were going to sleep for a month."

"You mean I didn't?"

"Not quite. It's a good thing you finally woke up; after a week we throw you out in the street to make room for the next wounded. How do you feel?"

"In the order of intensity, I feel thirsty, groggy, my left leg hurts, and my right foot itches." The nurse, whose name was Susan, but to a marine corporal she would be Lieutenant Jones, poured him a glass of water, "I can get you a glass of water but I can't do anything about the rest of it. The doctor has to prescribe something for the pain; he'll be along soon. It is funny how something that isn't there can itch, isn't it?" Alarm bells started sounding in Smitty's head. "What do you mean, 'that isn't there'?" Sue realized then that the corporal didn't know what had happened to him. Being as tender hearted as a Navy nurse in a combat zone can be she replied, "I'm sorry, marine. I didn't know that you didn't know but you have lost your right foot."

"It can't be lost. It itches."

"I'm sorry, but it's like that sometimes. It's like your brain won't admit that it's gone. I know it doesn't make sense that something can itch that isn't there." He tried to sit up, but was too weak, and fell back. "I would like to see it, Lieutenant." She moved the covers back off of his leg, and lifted it up so he could see. The look on his face changed from curiosity, to anger then to sadness. He looked at the nurse, nodded his head, then laid back on the pillow and stared at the ceiling, not saying anything. The doctor came in later, told the nurse to get him something to eat and to give him some pain killers for his other leg. When that was all taken care of, Smitty went back to sleep.

It was night when he woke up again. He was glad of that. He didn't want to talk to anybody. He needed time to think. "What am I going to do now?" He ran every day that he was not in the jungle playing war. He had to in order to stay in shape for the love of his life: tennis. He was the singles champion of the division and planned to join a semi-pro tennis club when he got out of the Marines. He had been saving all the money he could while he was in the service, so that he would have enough to live on until he could make it as a pro tennis champ. He told himself, "Now all that is finished; you can't be a pro with only one foot." He lay there thinking about the year he had just spent in Vietnam and about the time he won the medal for carrying those five guys out of danger in the middle of a fire fight when he was the radio operator for the forward observer. He and the F.O. were in a fox hole right behind the front lines. They were in the middle of calling in mortar missions when Smitty looked over the edge of the fox hole to see the enemy coming in force out of the jungle ahead of them. He pulled his rifle up and started firing along with the others in the fox holes in front of his position. By the time the attack broke, there were a lot of wounded around them. They called in a mortar mission on the jungle in front of them. They figured that they would be under attack again as soon as the mortars quit firing. Smitty slipped over edge of the hole and started lifting the wounded to his shoulder and carrying them back away from the front. He got five wounded out of there before the attack came again.

Someone moaned down the line of beds. A couple of other guys were snoring. They must have moved him into a ward while he was asleep. He was lying there thinking gloomy thoughts about sitting in a wheel chair with his right pants leg pinned up, begging for change, when he fell asleep again.

After he had been there a week, The Brick showed up

for a visit. He walked up to Smitty's bed, "Hello, Smitty. Have you got a date with a pretty nurse yet?"

"No, none of them wants to go out with a one legged man. Besides I haven't even made it out of this bed to shit yet."

"Well, you always were full of shit; it must be worse than usual now."

"How about yanking me out of bed and dragging to the outhouse? I'm tired of those bed pans and having some corpsman wiping my ass all the time."

"Sure. Let me go find a wheelchair; you're too heavy to carry." The process went pretty well; The Brick soon had Smitty back in bed.

"Whew, what a rush; I got a little dizzy at first, but it was good to be out of bed for a while."

"Whew, what a smell; I could tell you hadn't been out of bed for a while."

The Brick came every day for a week. On the last day he told Smitty, "I'm leaving for the states the day after tomorrow so I won't see you till you get sent over there. Here is the address of my new duty station. When you land over there, send me a note, and I'll come see you." Smitty said, "Sure." But he was thinking "Why would you want to visit a cripple?"

A few days later, the word came down that they were shipping a bunch of the more badly wounded stateside. The nurse, Lt. Sue, came to tell him that he was on the list. "Guess what, marine. You are going home. They are sending you to the Long Beach Naval Hospital. They have a special unit there that will fit you with a peg leg so that you can go back to chasing women again."

"Thank you for the news, Lieutenant, but with a peg leg I will only be able to catch the slow ones, and they are either old, fat, or ugly." She chuckled a little. "Oh, Smitty, you are such a sweetheart that a missing foot won't make any difference. I'd marry you myself if I wasn't already married." Smitty just looked down, thinking for a minute, then looked up, smiled and said, "Thank you, Lieutenant, you are a very nice lady, and I believe what you say but I'm pretty sure the only reason a woman would have anything to do with me would be out of pity and I don't want any of that."

"You wait and see. Once you get used to that peg leg nobody will know that you have one until you take your clothes off. I've seen you with them off, so I'm sure that that wooden foot won't make any difference after she has seen what else you've got." The men in the beds around close had been listening, and everyone broke out laughing. Smitty turned a dark shade of red under his tan; Lt. Sue just smiled and left.

A week later he was in a Hospital in Long Beach, California, where they elect movie stars as governors. As soon as Smitty got settled in, he sent a card to The Brick, telling him where he was and asking him to come rescue him from the boredom of the hospital routine. He knew that The Brick was not due back from his thirty-day leave for another two weeks, so he was surprised to see him come strolling in that Friday afternoon. "I didn't expect to see you for a couple of weeks. How come you're back early?" The Brick got a sour look on his face, "You know that I sent all that money home for my dad to save for me so I could buy a car when I got home. Well, he spent most of it. All he could come up with was three hundred and I had to threaten his life to get that much."

"How come he spent it?"

"Ah, my younger sister was having some problems so he gave it to her. You know her; she's a mental case. She will always be having trouble. I can't afford to be bailing her out all the time but it seems I'm a rotten guy for not wanting to. Anyway, I only stayed a week and came back here. I found a pretty good car on a lot outside the base. It has a base sticker on it, so I don't have to go through all that inspection stuff." The Brick drove his car around to the entrance for outpatients; Smitty hobbled out on his crutches and they headed for the Hollywood freeway. The Brick had heard of an Irish bar named Sullivan's where there were always a bunch of guys around a piano singing Irish songs. Smitty's only comment was, "Imagine that." The Brick got Smitty into a chair near the piano and ordered them each a beer. By the end of the evening they were good friends with everybody there, even the guy who took a swing at The Brick for flirting with the waitress, which didn't go well at all for the swinger as The Brick is one tough guy. It didn't matter to the Irishmen there who won the fight. They just loved the sport of it. They have a saying at that bar: if you haven't seen a good fight by ten o'clock, start one.

Smitty felt a little left out. Now he knew what it was like to be the one legged man at an ass kicking contest. They left there about midnight, and went to a bar where there were a lot of girls. The Brick is a pretty good looking dude even with his busted looking nose. He was dancing with one girl after another, but Smitty couldn't dance. In fact he was kind of a wet blanket the whole weekend. When they got back to the hospital The Brick helped Smitty out of the car, onto his crutches, and reminded him, "I'll pick you up next Friday and we'll do it again."

"No, it isn't much fun just watching you have fun. Stop by and say hi on your way out on Friday, but you will have more fun without me around."

"Well, aren't we feeling sorry for ourselves? I'll just come by on Sunday and tell you about all the Irishmen I hit, and all the girls I hugged. Then you'll be sorry you didn't go. Besides, you were a lousy dancer when you had two feet, and you were too nice a guy to ever get into a fight so what did you miss out on?"

Smitty smiled. "I think it's the idea that I couldn't even if I wanted to."

The Brick stopped by every Friday, but left without Smitty. He would return every Sunday and tell Smitty about fighting ten Irishmen at a time and having to juggle dates with five girls each weekend. After six weeks of that Smitty asked him, "Brick, don't you know that it's a sin to lie?"

"Yes, but I made a deal with God that if I told them so big that no one believed them I wouldn't have to confess them."

The Navy finally got around to fitting Smitty with a plastic foot. The first time he tried to walk on it, it hurt like hell. When he complained, the doctor said that it would quit hurting after the stump toughened up but that he needed to keep doing it or it would never quit hurting; he stumped around the hospital until he could get around with a cane. When the Brick came the next Friday, he agreed to go with him. As they were driving to Hollywood, Smitty told him, "I got the word that they are tired of paying me for doing nothing so they are kicking me out."

"What are you going to do?"

"I'm going home to see my dad for a few weeks. I wrote and told him what day I would be flying in and to meet me at the airport. After that, I think I'll take all that money I've been saving and buy a little cabin out in the woods, where I can now and then shoot a deer from my front porch,"

"When you get all settled in, write to me; I'll come sit on your front porch with you. Be careful when you go home, though; the hippies have been hanging around the airports harassing the vets as they come home. You better wear civvies"

"I think that it would be just fine to run into some of those draft dodging jerks. The mood I'm in, I would love to knock a little patriotism into twenty or thirty of them. The Brick agreed. "Boy, I would really like to be there to help."

The weekend went well. Smitty danced a little, but stayed aloof. He didn't want to get involved with any of these Hollywood type girls. They all wanted you to be rich and famous, and he had no plans to do anything to get rich.

Anyway, it was his last weekend in Southern California.

The day came for him to fly home; it's not a long flight from L.A. to Seattle. He could have gone on to Spokane; it would have been a little shorter drive for his dad, but his dad liked to go to the big city once in a while. They had talked on the phone that morning about going to the wharf, Pike St. market, and the space needle; it would be fun to do that with the old man again. It was too bad, he was thinking, that his mom wasn't still alive to go with them.

In those days you still had to walk from the plane to the terminal, and anybody could walk out to meet you. There were seven men in uniform on this flight, including himself, a couple on crutches and another marine with a cane. Smitty saw a couple of airline people carry a soldier who had both legs amputated down the steps and into a waiting wheelchair. A small crowd of forty or fifty anti-war demonstrators were lining up to form a gauntlet for the servicemen getting off the plane. Smitty, knowing the old saying that words can never hurt you, had decided that he was not going to do anything about the jeers of the hippies who now blocked the way of all the disembarking passengers but then let the civilians through while still keeping the service personnel back. The guy in the wheelchair was out front and, even though the airline attendant was trying to get through, the crowd was not having any of it. Smitty turned to the other marine, a Sergeant, and asked, "Are we going to let this happen?"

"I can hardly walk; I wouldn't be much help."

"Then hold my cane for me so I won't be tempted to use it as a weapon." Smitty hobbled past the others; he got to the wheelchair just in time to witness two dirty looking creeps take turns spitting on the guy in the chair. Smitty stepped in front of the two, reached up and grabbed them by their long greasy hair and lifted them up onto their tippy toes and said, "I guess I had better teach you boys some respect for your betters." The hippie crowd didn't like that much and closed in. When a half full pop can hit Smitty on his left ear he bellowed, "That does it." He smacked those two heads together hard enough to hear them crack, dropped them, and proceeded to smack one face after another. He received a punch now and then but every time his big fists hit someone they went down. He knocked down anybody who got within reach. The fight was on.

His dad, who was on the outside of the crowd, saw what was happening, let out a roar and charged. Mr. Smith was just as big as Smitty. When he broke through the crowd, he yelled, "Let's get these stinking hippies, son." They were joined by the servicemen who weren't disabled and soon had a broad pathway cleared through the crowd except for a body here and there, but other than that it was clear. The hippies who were not as brave as their fellows were moving back out of the way when the airport security showed up. The two Mr. Smiths were out front, and the man in charge asked them, "Okay, what happened here?" Dumb question. Smith Sr. responded, "Oh nothing, officer, I just came to escort these fine men through that crowd of smelly humanity back there." The security guard said "I suppose those on the ground are taking a nap."

"Oh, some of them did trip and fall down getting out of our way, but they're all right. Come on, son, let's get your bags." The security guards, being a little tired of the demonstrators, and seeing that they were all getting back on their feet, moved out of the way and let them pass. One of the security men said, "Welcome home, marine, I'm glad to see you didn't lose your spirit while you were away."

When they arrived in Seattle, they drove down to the pier area by the ferry terminal to do the tourist thing. They bought some ice cream; Mr. Smith Sr. suggested, "Let's sit over here on the bench and eat these things and talk. You haven't said much since we left the airport. Did that special welcoming party upset you, son?"

"Yes it did. I don't care if those yellow bellies don't go fight for their country but that's no way to treat the guys that did. I'd like to take a machine gun to them. Did you see them spit on that guy with no legs?"

"Yes I did. It made me very angry, too, but I worked out most of my anger by punching them in the face. Maybe you're mad just because I hit more of them than you did. Come on, try to put all that out of your mind for now and let's have a good time today."

CHAPTER THREE

Before they left the airport, Smitty cleaned up and changed into his civilian clothes. He didn't really want to fight every anti-war nut that he ran into; there were just too many of them around those days. Sooner or later, one of them would complain to the cops and he might end up in the slammer. He had let his hair grow out while he was in the hospital. With a nice pair of gray slacks, a blue and gray bulky knit sweater, and a pair of great looking loafers, he didn't look military anymore. No matter how much his dad cleaned up, he still looked like a farmer.

They went through the shops in the pier area, rode

the old trolley, had lunch, and toured the Pike Street market. Smitty's leg was beginning to hurt so they took a cab to the space needle. When they got to the top and had looked around a little while, Smitty told his dad that he was ready to head for the old homestead. Mr. Smith took one more look at the Seattle skyline. "Yes, I guess we have about worn out our welcome here and it's a long drive home.

Going over the pass on I-90, Mr. Smith asked, "Do you have any idea what you are going to do, now that you are out, Wayne?" Smitty didn't answer right away as he knew that his dad wasn't going to like his answer. He finally turned to him, "Well, with only one leg I wouldn't be any help on the farm, and I can't play tennis, so I think I will become a hermit. The Brick and I went skiing at Lake Tahoe for a few days before we went to Nam and I fell in love with the area. I want to take the money I saved to start my tennis career and buy a place back in the mountains and grow a garden, hunt, fish, and try to live on my disability pay. The war took away my ability to do what I wanted to do, so I'm going to do the other thing that I always wanted to do when I retired."

"It sounds to me like you just want to go away and sulk."

"I guess it would sound like that to you; you still have both of your legs." They were both quiet for a while, then

Smitty continued, "You know, you could sell the farm and come, too. We would have a good time fishing and hunting together. And I am not going to just sulk. When I'm not fishing, I think I would like to write a book." His Dad looked at him like he had just turned a bright shade of green. When he got the truck straightened out, he said, "I forgot that you learned how to write before you went away. What are you going to write about?"

"Everybody has been telling about all the bad things that happened over there in Nam. I think someone should tell about the good things we did there. Anyway, I could write a whole stack of books on the stories The Brick has told me. That guy is more full of crap than anybody I ever met. The funny thing is, he makes them sound believable."

It was late by the time they got to the farm so they went right to bed. Mr. Smith was up early. He woke Smitty by yelling up the stairs, "Hey, breakfast is ready. Wake up and smell the coffee." While they were eating Mr. Smith continued the conversation begun the night before. "I have been thinking over what you said yesterday. Maybe you had a good idea about me selling the farm. I have been thinking about retiring for the last couple of years. While you're home, how about helping me do some fixing up, and we can put it on the market and head for Californ-i-a?"

Because of the kind of man Mr. Smith was, there wasn't much fixing up to do. By the end of the week they had everything done so Mr. Smith suggested, "How about having a party, sort of a welcome home-going away type of shindig combined. What do you say?" Smitty didn't want to have all the neighbors over, asking a lot of stupid questions like, "How did you like the war, son?" or "You didn't kill any women or children while you were over there, did you, Wayne?" He was about to tell his dad no when he remembered how much the old man liked to have the neighbors over for a get together so he gave in. "Sure, Pop, but tell them not to bug me about the leg, okay?" The old man laughed, and asked, "When are you going get over being touchy about that peg?

"Maybe when it quits hurting so much."

By the time Saturday night rolled around Smitty was sure that everybody in the county had been invited and told to bring finger food which, to a farmer's wife, meant anything edible that will fit in the back of a pickup truck. A lot of people showed up with enough food to feed a whole company of Marines. Smitty had to admit that it was nice to see all the friendly faces again. When everyone got settled down, after the howdys and all, Mr. Smith yelled to get everyone's attention, "I know that you all came here tonight to welcome Wayne home from the Marines." Everyone clapped, and cheered. "And to eat. Thank you everyone for all the food." More noise. "Now we have a little news for you. You know that it has always been my wish for Wayne to take over the farm when I got too old. He has decided that he doesn't want to be a peg legged farmer, so we are going to sell the farm and move to California." Now there was a lot of yelling and groaning, and asking of questions. The old man raised his hands to quiet the crowd, "I know we have been here a long time and we will miss you, too. Wayne has decided that he wants to be a writer of books. We are going to find a place back in the woods near Lake Tahoe. That way he can have a little privacy, and I can get to know some of those show girls in Reno."

Before the party was over, Mr. Carson, who lived on the farm next door, came to Mr. Smith and informed him, "I'd like to buy your place from you, Don, if you are not asking too much. My oldest son just got married and they need a house to move into. With the extra mouths to feed, we can use the extra acres, too." The two old men went into the den, kicked out a couple of teenagers who were kissing and hugging, and worked out a deal on the farm.

CHAPTER FOUR

The next weekend found them loading the pickup. They left most of the old stuff for the newlyweds. The truck was mostly loaded with shop tools. They had worked hard that day so they didn't make it too far before they stopped to sleep. The motel they stopped at had a bar and restaurant, so after they put their gear in their room, they ate, and stopped in at the bar for a drink before bedding down for the night. Once they had their drinks in their hands, Mr. Smith said, "You know, I am really looking forward to this. We can find us a nice little place on the edge of town, with a nice place for a garden and I'll be happy for the rest of my life."

"That sounds great, Dad. After we get you all settled in on the edge of town, I'll start looking for my place out in the boonies so I can start being a hermit."

"I was hoping that you were kidding about that."

"I'm only twenty two years old, and some day some girl will feel sorry enough for me to ask me to marry her and I would like to have a place of my own fixed up the way I want it when that happens."

After looking all over the area, Mr. Smith found a cozy two bedroom place on the outskirts of Reno, really nearer to Carson City. They spent a few days moving, which required buying some furniture to replace the stuff that was left behind. Once that was done they started looking for a place for Smitty. They did the normal house hunting routine, going through the real estate listings, then the for-sale-by-owner listings in the newspapers. After about four days of this they stopped in a restaurant for some pie and coffee and to go over the list of the properties Smitty liked; his dad hoped, "Maybe you can talk yourself into buying one of them." It was a nice old, roomy, restaurant in the little town of Tahoe Pines on the west side of the lake. It was built of logs with a shiny new blue metal roof. The place smelled of good cooking, and the people were friendly. They found themselves an out of the way booth and the old man took the note pad and laid it on the table. He had written down the address, phone number, price and description of all the places that were even close to what Smitty was looking for. Some of them were just acreages. Most of them had some kind of house on them, but most of those were just shacks. While Smitty was reading through the descriptions, Mr. Smith commented, "All of the places looked good to me; some of them needed a lot of work though. I think you would be better off in the long run buying one of the better places. You would end up spending about the same amount of money fixing up one of the cheaper places." The waitress walked up during that conversation. "I'm sorry for eavesdropping but what kind of place are you looking for?"

"I'm looking for a place on the edge of nowhere, like a hunting cabin." Mr. Smith said, "He thinks he wants to be a hermit." Then he rolled his eyes up to the decorations around the ceiling. Smitty frowned at his dad. The girl smiled. "I know a place for sale like that. It's cheap, too. It's a log house, on ten acres that backs up to the national forest. It has a little creek running through it.

"That sounds like what I'm looking for. What do they want for it?"

"Eight thousand." Smitty looked at his list. "That's

better than we have found so far, by a bunch. What's the cabin like?"

"It's a chalet type. The downstairs is the kitchen, dining and front room all in one open room. The upstairs has a ladder up to it. It is just a big open sleeping area, with windows at each end." As she described the cabin, her voice got kind of sad. Mr. Smith looked at her, smiled, and said, "No electricity, or running water, and an outhouse, right?" She looked at the floor, "Yes, and it's my house, and I really need to sell it." Smitty smiled and said, "That sounds like the kind of place I'm looking for. How do we find it? She was astonished. "I could show you, but I don't get off for three hours, and it's hard to find." Mr. Smith encouraged her with, "The place doesn't look that busy; come show us." Smitty added, "You go square it with your boss. If you can't afford to take the time off, here's twenty bucks for guide service. Before you go though, you better get Dad some pie and coffee. He's still a growing boy, you know."

CHAPTER FIVE

The apple pie was great. By the time they finished it and the coffee, the girl was ready to go. Once out in the parking lot, they introduced themselves. Her name was Amanda Jones. Mr. Smith said something about Alias Smith and Jones, and they all climbed into the truck for a guided tour of the mountains. They went south along the highway on the west side of the lake for about four miles, then turned off on a dirt road that wound back into the mountains. They passed a few scattered houses on the way. The first of these were pretty nice but they got smaller and shabbier as they got further away from the lake. The road went up and down hills, twisted and turned for miles back into the woods. The forest was mostly fir and pine. Occasionally there was one of those huge mountain oaks. It was just the type of place Smitty was looking for. They saw a dozen deer in a nearby meadow. They even forded a small creek. It seemed like a long time since they had passed the last house when they came to a pole fence. There were tall gate posts with a log for a top piece with *Lazy Acres* carved into it. The woods were too thick to see the cabin from the road. Amanda told Mr. Smith to turn in at the gate and go down the slightly sloping drive.

They rounded a bend in the drive and came upon the cabin. Mr. Smith stopped the truck, and muttered, "I expect Davey Crocket to step out at any minute." Just then a teenage girl came out with a baby on her hip, and a five year old boy by the hand. They got out of the truck and Amanda introduced them to her kids. She took them on a tour of the place, first to the outhouse which was next to a wood shed which contained enough room for six cord, then to the creek below the cabin, where they got their water. Next they toured the cabin. It was one big room, built of logs on a solid foundation of mortar and stone. The roof was steep enough that it would shed snow and create space enough for an upstairs. The only way up was a ladder through a trap door in the ceiling. Smitty struggled up the ladder to find two bedrooms with just the basic furniture. The rafters were of large logs with rough lumber above and no insulation. He climbed down again and Amanda showed them the kitchen; it was an add-on with a gas range. "The refrigerator is even gas. Don't ask me how it works, but it does. The hand pump at the sink works most of the time. If we have a dry year it will run out by the end of August."

Amanda was pretty sure that Smitty wasn't going to buy the place. It wasn't anything he said; he hadn't said anything. The old man's comments were all negative such as, "What, no musket over the door?" Or, "Where is the bear rug?" She was feeling pretty disappointed so she told them she needed to get back to work. "Do you guys know anybody with some wheels who would drive me?" On the way back to town, much to Amanda's surprise, Smitty said, "I like the place, but I need to talk to your husband. I would need to know where the corners are, and talk about how much down and so on."

"We need three thousand down. It's what we need for the down on the house in town that we want. As far as my husband goes, he works nights so if you tell me when you want to see him I'll make sure he's home."

That night, back at the old man's house, Mr. Smith

mused, "I could tell that you really liked that place but it really needs a lot of work. Are you going to have enough money left, after you make the down payment, to fix everything that needs to be fixed?"

"Like what? I like it the way it is."

"Like a bathroom, and a septic system, and some running water. Maybe even a wind generator for some electricity. Besides that, you're going to have to buy a four wheel drive rig with a plow on it to get out of there in the winter. That's like what."

"Okay, let's make a list of what you think I need and estimate the cost. Then we'll see how much you'll need to give me to get it all done."

"Give you, who said I was going to give you anything?" the old tight wad shouted.

Once they had it down on paper, subtracting out what Smitty had in the bank, he was going to need close to eight thousand to do it all. Mr. Smith said, "Well, I had it all set up in my will that your older brother was going to get the farm, and you and your sister weren't getting anything." Smitty just smiled, knowing the old man was yanking his chain. "But," the old man continued, "now that I sold the farm, I have decided to split the money between you boys, and leave my house to your sister. I will give you ten thousand now and adjust my will accordingly. You will need furniture and a lot of other things."

"That's great, Dad. Thanks. As far as furniture goes I was just going to take yours."

The next day, after breakfast at Amanda's restaurant, Smitty and his dad drove out to meet Amanda's husband. They walked the property, were told lots of stories about the country, and when Smitty told him of his plans, Jim told him that a neighbor had a backhoe that he could borrow if he knew how to run it. Jim also told them that if Smitty was going to live there year around he would need a four wheel drive rig and that he would sell him his, with the plow, for five hundred bucks. So by the end of the day things were looking pretty good.

CHAPTER SIX

With his dad's help the work went pretty fast. Not only did Smitty get everything done by the next winter but all the work helped him adjust to his peg leg. He didn't limp anymore. They borrowed the backhoe, found a spring up the hill from the cabin, put in a spring box, dug a ditch, buried a water line to the house from the spring, and then put in a septic system. They excavated for the footings for an addition on the side of the house thereby adding a master bedroom, a bathroom, and a laundry/mud room. They built a set of stairs replacing the ladder and the trap door. They also got rid of the outhouse.

The house changed from a square box with a front room, kitchen, and dining area, downstairs with space for two bedrooms upstairs to a nice little three bedroom house, with indoor plumbing. Smitty had a wind generator put in. His dad wired the house so that he could have some lights and a few small appliances while Smitty did a lot of finish work that really made the place look great. By the end of September the house was done. The two Smiths spent time cutting firewood for both houses, preparing for the long mountain winter.

One day Smitty informed his dad, "I heard on the radio last night that there is a big gun show in Reno this weekend. We have never gone hunting together. What say we mosey over to the big city and buy some weapons to go shoot a Bambi or two?"

"Sounds great. We could set up a range out here to sight them in, and fill up our freezers."

"We don't have a freezer but I have been thinking of getting one, and a TV, too, now that I have electricity."

Saturday morning Smitty ate breakfast at Amanda's restaurant. She came to wait on him and asked, "Well, Smitty, how is the house coming?"

"It's pretty much all done. I am headed for Reno to buy a freezer and TV."

"You have electricity?"

"Yes, I had a wind generator put in. They told me it was enough for the basics. You and the family should come see the place sometime."

"An indoor toilet, running water, and a wash machine?"

"Yep, real up town. Come see."

"I will, but it will probably make me cry."

When he picked up his dad he told him about talking with Amanda. "Amanda and Jim and the kids are coming over tomorrow night for a pot luck dinner. You are bringing the drinks. No one wanted to eat any of your cooking."

After driving around a bit, they found the gun show. Smitty bought a Marlin 30-30 with a scope, and a nice case. Then a guy talked him into a compound bow and, at a table full of handguns, he bought a Dan Wesson 357 in a holster. He was all set. They went to a sporting goods store, bought some ammo, and arrows, and other stuff; from there they moved on to an appliance store for the freezer and the biggest TV they had. On the way out of town they stopped at a stationary store for a typewriter so Smitty could begin his first book.

When they came out of the store, a teenage girl was standing on the sidewalk with a half grown St. Bernard puppy on a leash sitting beside her. She begged, "Would one of you guys like to have a puppy?" They both laughed. Mr. Smith said, "I don't think we could afford to feed it. If that's a puppy, how big will he be when he's full grown?"

"I don't know. He's six months old and the last of the pups. We sold all the rest, but no one wanted him. Mom said to give him away since we can't afford to feed him anymore." Smitty put the typewriter on the backseat of his truck, reached down and petted the dog who licked his hand and looked up at him with big sad eyes and woofed. It was a woof. A big woof, not a bark. Smitty asked her, "What's his name?"

"Sherpa, you know, after the Everest guides."

"That's cute. Okay, I'll take him." Now they had to make one more stop to get a couple hundred pounds of dog food, and all the other junk that goes with a dog. While he was at it, he bought the biggest sled dog harness they had. He figured Sherpa was going to have to work for a living. A little bit anyway.

The next few months went by quickly. Smitty and his slobbery mouthed friend explored all the mountains and valleys around, moving out further and camping out for longer periods on each trip. Sherpa took right to pulling a military cargo sled full of camping gear once the snow was on the ground. Smitty and his Dad each got a deer, and they caught a lot of fish. By the time winter set in in earnest, they had both of their freezers full of meat. Amanda and Jim invited them over for Thanksgiving dinner, and talked of nothing but how they liked all the things that Smitty had done to his place.

Smitty started working on his book, which would be a little different than most. It was about the good things that were happening in Nam. Most writers just told about the killing. He wanted to tell about the housing for the refugees, or building orphanages and roads through the jungle between cities.

Sherpa didn't like being in the house; it was too hot for a big fur coat. When Smitty let him in, he would only be in for a few minutes before he would be standing at the door panting and wanting out so whenever Smitty took a break from his writing, he would pull on a parka and go out and sit on the covered porch with his new pal. It was better that way; in the warm house that dog could slobber a gallon of water an hour which was a mess to clean up off those hardwood floors.

At the end of the third week of December, when Smitty went out to feed Sherpa his breakfast, he discovered two feet of snow that wasn't there when he went to bed. "Well, young feller, I guess we had better clear the road. We could use a few groceries, and we need to check the mail, too."

It was still snowing so he took his time eating and cleaning up before he went out. He was hoping it would quit, but it didn't look like it was going to. He shoveled a path out to the truck, then cleared an area around the truck for a parking space; it was still snowing. He opened the tail gate for Sherpa to jump in. Sherpa liked riding back there, and it didn't matter where he slobbered on the truck bed. He plowed the right side of the road on his way out; he would get the other side on the way back. Before he got to the mail boxes he ran out of road to plow as some early bird had got there ahead of him. It had been a little slow going at the ford in the creek. Next summer he would have to build a bridge over that creek, and a garage too. He stopped to pick up his mail as he went by. Mostly junk. He would read the good stuff at Amanda's restaurant while he ate lunch.

When Amanda came to take his order, he asked her, "How is the most beautiful waitress of the west?"

"Thank you, Smitty. I'm fine. How are you?"

"Doing good. Will it quit snowing someday soon?"

"You can't start complaining yet; it's not even Christmas. Don't you know it's against the law up here to complain about the snow until the end of January?"

"Well, my back hurts from all the shoveling; I like

the snow except when I have to shovel it." She took his order, and left. While he was waiting for his lunch, he sorted through the mail; there was quite a pile. Maybe he should pick it up more often. All of a sudden one of them made him smile; it was from The Brick. He had written The Brick a couple of letters, telling him about his place, and hunting, and fishing, and his dog. He got a post card back: "sounds great. The Brick." He skimmed down through the crap about the fights and the girls to the good stuff. The Brick said that he had two weeks leave and was going to come spend it with him. He would arrive at the Reno airport December 22, at 4:00 p.m. Smitty thought: Great. Now I will have to put up a tree and buy him a present. The Brick would never think to ask if it would fit into his plans or not; he would just show up. Oh well, it would be good to see him. The old man had been checking out the shows at the casinos in Reno, it would be fun to get him to take them to a couple of shows. It would give The Brick a lot of stories to tell when he got back to the base, some of them might even be true.

When Amanda brought his lunch, he asked, "What's the date today?"

"The twent-first, why?"

"I have a buddy coming in tomorrow to spend a couple of weeks and I just found out about it." She looked down at the big pile of mail on the table, smiled and said, "You should pick up your mail more often."

Smitty rushed around town buying stuff, called his dad, told him the news, and made arrangements for him to go to the airport with him. He finished plowing the other side of the road on the way home, and plowed a big parking area at the house. The rest of the day was spent going out in the deep snow with Sherpa to cut a small tree, decorating it and wrapping presents for his dad and The Brick. There was even a big leather bone for Sherpa.

In the morning, he cleaned house, made up a bed in one of the upstairs bedrooms, stoked up the wood stove, and then closed the damper so that it would still be burning when they got back. When he went out, he fed Sherpa and chained him up. He didn't think he would do too well at the Reno airport. The snow had stopped with only a few inches of new stuff where he had plowed. He stopped at the mail box, but there was nothing there today. He picked up his dad, and they headed for Reno. As they were driving Smitty noticed that his dad was dressed very nicely, wearing an overcoat, instead of a heavy jacket. He decided not to say anything, but it did seem strange. They ate lunch at one of the small casinos on the edge of town.

While they were eating, Smitty said, "I know that you

have been checking out the show girls in town here so how about taking us to a show tonight? The Brick would think that was great, and I would like to see one, too."

"I know just the one; we have time so let's pick up the tickets on the way to the airport."

They parked in the waiting area at the airport, out of the cold, watching people coming and going. The Brick came through the door with a big grin on his face. Smitty said, "Oh brother, he's in uniform."

"So what? It just shows that he isn't ashamed of being a jarhead."

"He just does that to get the anti-war hippies excited so he can smack them around."

"Sounds like my kind of guy."

The Brick spotted them and came over with an indignant look on his face. "You should have seen that out there. I was accosted by four hippies." Mr. Smith asked, "Did you leave any of them standing?"

"No, but they'll be okay in a week or two so let's get my sea bag and go see the town."

They picked up The Brick's bag, but Smitty made him change into civilian clothes before they left the airport. The Brick, being from the flat lands, didn't have a heavy coat, but Smitty had brought one for him. His shirt was a little wrinkled but he looked good with the coat on. Smitty instructed him with, "We are taking you to some nice places and we don't want you to get us thrown out for starting fights or for looking ragged." Mr. Smith added, "It's a sad situation in this country when one of our military men has to be ashamed of his uniform."

"Yeah, real sad." said The Brick.

They had tickets for a later show so they went to have dinner at a different club. After dinner, The Brick wanted to play black jack; the old man started playing the wheel of fortune. After a while Smitty began trying to herd The Brick and his dad out of the casino. "Come on, Brick, we better get going."

"Oh sure, I have to leave when I'm ahead. If I quit when I'm ahead, I won't have any long sad tales to tell when I get back to the base."

He picked up his money and they went over to where the old man was. The Brick counted his money and discovered that he was about fifty bucks ahead. Smitty went over to the old man. "It's about time to go, Dad." Mr. Smith turned and whispered, "See that guy standing back a ways over there? He only plays every once in a while, but he wins almost every time." The Brick said, "The next time he plays, I'm putting all my winnings on what he does." Mr. Smith kept playing where he was. Smitty moved over closer to where the man was standing and started playing. In a few minutes, the man moved up to the table and placed some money on the five to one. The Brick, who was standing next to Mr. Smith, put his winnings on the five to one; the two Smiths each put down a twenty. They watched as the wheel spun and started to slow down. The Brick leaned over to Mr. Smith, "If I lose, I will probably have to walk back to the base." The wheel came to a stop. Of course it was the five to one. You wouldn't want our friends to lose, would you?

CHAPTER SEVEN

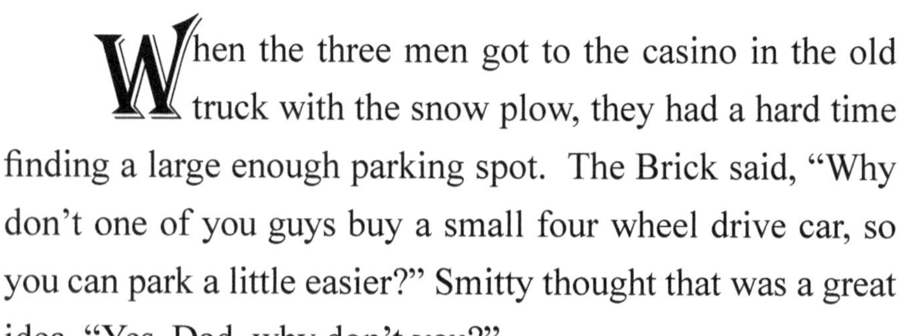

When the three men got to the casino in the old truck with the snow plow, they had a hard time finding a large enough parking spot. The Brick said, "Why don't one of you guys buy a small four wheel drive car, so you can park a little easier?" Smitty thought that was a great idea. "Yes, Dad, why don't you?"

"Why me?"

"Because I'm about broke. I'm going to have to actually start living on my rocking chair money."

When they got to the head waiter's little stand the man behind it looked up; "Ah, Mr. Smith, it's good to see you again. Please follow me. I have a great table for you." He took them to a table in the center of the room and close to the stage. The head waiter was tipped, a waiter took their orders for drinks and left. Smitty leaned over to The Brick, and whispered, "What do you make of dad getting all dressed up for tonight?" The Brick looked over at Mr. Smith, "Well, sir, I am glad that you finally realized how important I am and dressed properly for the great occasion of my coming to town." Both of the Smiths laughed, but the show started just then, before Smitty had a chance to comment.

They all enjoyed the show. It was a great show, but Smitty noticed that his dad had eyes for only one show girl. When the show was over, The Brick said, "Let's go hit another casino. I feel lucky tonight." Mr. Smith said, "Don't get in a hurry; I have a surprise for you. Just finish your drinks and relax for a minute." Now Smitty knew why the old man got all dressed up for tonight. "You should have warned us, Dad; now I know why you are wearing your finest." The Brick didn't get it. "You do look like you are either marrying or burying someone. What's up?" For his answer Mr. Smith stood up and smiled as three lovely women stopped at their table. "Hello. You girls did a great job tonight, the best yet. Okay girls, pick your guys." The older one looked around at all three men, like she was trying to decide which one to pick.

"I guess I'll take the well dressed old guy; he's probably got the most money. By the way, since Don forgot to introduce us, I'm Ginger. This pretty blond is Sue, and the cute little brunette is Shannon." The Brick broke in with, "I'm John, this big hulk is Don's son, Wayne, but everyone calls him Smitty. And I love cute little brunettes named Shannon." Everyone laughed; Smitty said, "Well, Sue, I guess you are stuck with me tonight."

"Good," Sue said, as she smiled up at Smitty. "You look like a nice little man." Ginger said, "If he's as big as his dad, he's not little." Even though the two Smiths looked a little uncomfortable, the evening looked like it would be fun. Before they could sit down, Sue suggested, "Let's go into the ballroom; I for one would like to dance." The Brick looked at Smitty and asked, "Can you dance?"

"You just watch me. In fact, I bet I don't step on Sue's toe as often as you step on Shannon's." And so they danced and talked the night away. By the end of the evening, it was obvious that The Brick was falling in love with Shannon, and that Mr. Smith had a thing going with Ginger. It looked like Sue and Smitty were getting along fine until she found out that he was an unpublished writer living on disability in a log cabin way out in the woods. Even though that information cooled her enthusiasm, they all agreed to do it again tomorrow night.

On the drive home The Brick asked, "Where are we staying tonight?"

"After we drop dad off, we'll go on out to my place. I thought you'd like to see it since I did all that fixing up just for your coming."

"That was real nice of you but I think I would like to stay in town tonight. I would like to buy something for a certain young lady before our date tomorrow night."

"Or," Mr. Smith said, "we could all come in early and do some shopping on our way to the show. We could ask the girls to come out to your place for Christmas. How about that?" And so it was agreed .

Smitty dropped his dad off and drove the long drive to his house. Half way there The Brick ran out of stories and fell asleep. He woke up when they splashed through the ford at the creek. Smitty said, "Well, sleepy head, we're almost there. That's the house there." Through the trees you could see the lights. After they parked and got out, Smitty quietly spoke, "Hey Brick, listen." The Brick stopped and listened for a minute. "It's real quiet, Smitty, I don't hear a thing except the breeze in the trees."

Sherpa came out to the end of his chain and woofed at them. "Wow, Smitty, you said he was big, but I never would have believed it. How much does he weigh?"

"Over two hundred. I stood him up on the bathroom scale with his front feet on my shoulders but it is real hard to see the dial down through his legs."

When they were in the house The Brick dropped his sea bag on the floor and stood looking around. "Mr. Smith, this is real nice. Did you do all this?"

"Most of it. My dad did a lot, too. He did all of the wiring. I get free electricity, which is nice."

"Free?"

"Oh yes. The wind generator."

"That's a great idea. Is there even power out this far in the back country?"

"No. It ends about three miles down the road; they wanted me to pay for extending the lines. I could have bought five wind generators for that much."

In the morning after breakfast, they headed for town. This time, as they forded the creek and drove the rutted dirt road through the forest, The Brick was awake. "I can see why you like this country, Smitty. I can also see why you drive this old four wheeler. This fir and pine forest must be real beautiful anytime, but with the snow on everything it's breathtaking."

"Yes, you and I have seen a lot of this old globe

together, but this is the most beautiful. I don't ever want to leave it."

"It looks like you got everything a guy could want: great hunting and fishing, a great house in great country, a huge slobbery dog; all you need is a girl. What about Sue?"

"She's a real cutie all right but when she found out I lived in the back woods on disability she turned real cold. Besides, if she finds out about the peg leg, and figures out my prospects, she probably won't talk to me again." The Brick could see that even though Smitty was pretty happy with his life now, he was still bitter over what he had lost. "You wait until she sees your house. And when you sell a couple of books and the money starts rolling in she will come crawling."

CHAPTER EIGHT

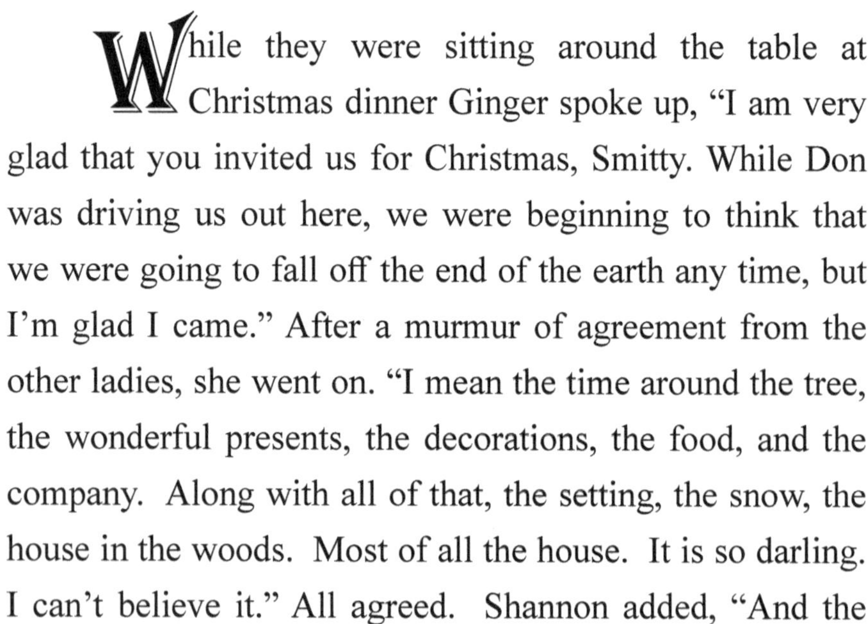

While they were sitting around the table at Christmas dinner Ginger spoke up, "I am very glad that you invited us for Christmas, Smitty. While Don was driving us out here, we were beginning to think that we were going to fall off the end of the earth any time, but I'm glad I came." After a murmur of agreement from the other ladies, she went on. "I mean the time around the tree, the wonderful presents, the decorations, the food, and the company. Along with all of that, the setting, the snow, the house in the woods. Most of all the house. It is so darling. I can't believe it." All agreed. Shannon added, "And the dog. He's big enough to saddle and ride. And so cute, and woolly."

The day went as all Christmas days should go with Christmas music playing on the stereo, the talk and atmosphere both cheery and nice. Everyone bundled up and walked up the road. Smitty slipped his 357 into his parka pocket in case they ran into some unfriendly critter that a two hundred pound St. Bernard couldn't handle. They walked along arm in arm as far as the ford in the creek, taking in the snowy winter wonderland. By the time they got back to the house, it was time for the girls to go. They had a show to do that night and it was a long way back to town. While everybody warmed up by the wood stove before leaving, Sue told Smitty, "Here is a little gift from me; they are tickets to the show. Anytime you can make it to town, you could come see the show for free and we could go dancing again. Thanks again for a great Christmas." Then she threw her arms around him and planted a huge sloppy kiss on him.

Mr. Smith stuck his head in the door to say the car was warmed up and ready to go; Sue and Ginger thanked Smitty again and went out. Shannon, still standing by the stove holding The Brick's hand, turned to Smitty and asked, "I can get next week off; can I come hang out with you guys? I would like to spend some time with John before he goes back to the base."

"Okay but there are two conditions. "

"Great. What are the two conditions?"

"One is separate bedrooms. I don't want any pregnant showgirl wanting to move in because she doesn't have any place to go and has a bum for a boyfriend who won't take care of her. The other is you have to talk The Brick into not eating so much while you're here. I'm not sure I can afford to feed a whole crowd for a week."

The Brick broke in with, "He has a freezer full of meat, and a root cellar full of veggies that he grew himself. This guy is so full of crap that you can never take him seriously." Shannon, standing between the two, looked a little nervous. Smitty, in a kind voice, said, "You are more than welcome to come stay here at any time and for as long as you want." Then he added with a smile, "Even if you are pregnant."

A time was set to pick her up in town, and she ran out to the car to leave for the long drive home. The two guys stood on the porch watching them go; each gave a little wave just before the car was out of sight, then headed into the house. They settled down with cups of hot coffee near the stove. The Brick said, "You know that for a nice guy you can be a real jerk sometimes. Pregnant showgirl? I plan to ask her to marry me while she's here next week"

"Don't worry about it. She seems to have more sense than that"

"I'm serious about this." The Brick looked troubled. "But there are a couple of problems. I'm going to need a job and a place to live."

"Reno is a big town. There should be lots of jobs."

"I don't really want to live and work in town. Can you think of anything out this way?"

"Well, there is a small sawmill for sale. The old guy who owns it wants to retire. But you would need some money."

"I have been thinking about getting out of the Corps ever since you moved up here. I have been saving as much as I could so I have a few thousand, but I don't know a thing about running a sawmill."

"I'm sure the old man would stick around for a while to show you the ropes. I think there are about twenty acres of land that go with it so you could build you a house right there." They talked about it as they cleaned up the Christmas dinner mess; the more they talked about it the more enthused they became.

After breakfast the next day, they drove over to talk to Mr. Mahan, the owner of the mill. He was a man in his sixties and as Irish as a shamrock. When Smitty introduced them he told Mr. Mahan that The Brick was half Irish himself, but that he wasn't any good at anything except drinking beer and telling lies. The old man responded, "Neither am I." When Sherpa woofed at them from the back of the truck Mr. Mahan said, "I see you brought my friend to see me. I think he's the only person in the whole county that likes old Irishmen." At a call from Smitty, Sherpa came over the side of the truck and ran to get petted.

They talked for a while. Smitty told the old man that The Brick was interested in buying the mill. He took them into the mill office and gave them a list of property and equipment that went with the mill. They discussed the price, down payment, and monthly payments. Mr. Mahan agreed to stay on for a while to show them the ropes, on the condition that Smitty would bring Sherpa along with him.

As they left the mill, The Brick told Smitty, "Man, that would be really great but how do I come up with that kind of money for a down payment?" Smitty headed the truck toward Reno. "We'll go see dad. If I go in as your partner, I'm sure he will loan us the money."

So when they went to pick up Shannon a couple of days later The Brick had a pretty good plan to present to her. On the way back to Smitty's after picking her up from her apartment, The Brick began the presentation. "You know

I'm up for reenlistment the end of next month. Well, I have decided to get out instead, and move up here." Shannon smiled, looked at him and said, "That's great, John. I could see that you were all excited about something. Have you been making plans?"

"You won't even believe it. We are on our way right now to put a deposit on a piece of land on which I am going to build a house. And as far as a job goes, Smitty and I are going to make little wooden things to sell." Smitty chuckled but said nothing. Shannon studied his face. "Okay, John, you have a big secret; do you plan to tell me someday?" Smitty said, "I think he is so excited that he won't be able to keep it in very long."

"The Brick said, "I have never owned anything before. Besides, the whole thing is so wonderful that I can't believe it is happening to me."

When they pulled up in front of the mill, he jumped out of the truck and ran up the steps into the office then right back out again to yell at Smitty, "Don't forget the paperwork." Mr. Mahan came out of the office. "I hope he is this excited when it comes time to do the work." They all laughed. Smitty introduced Shannon to Mr. Mahan. The paperwork was completed. The Brick and Shannon began walking all over the place with him showing her the mill, the equipment, the property, and asking her advice on where to build the house.

As they sat at dinner that night at Smitty's, Shannon asked, "So you two are going to make little wooden things, like lumber? And where did you two bums get enough money to even make a down payment on a place like that?"

The Brick answered, "We went to the National Bank of Don Smith. Not only did he loan us the money; he offered to help build the house and work at the mill. He paid the whole down payment. He told me to save the money I had for working on the house. What a guy."

After dinner Shannon and the Brick said they would get the dishes; Smitty said he was going to take Sherpa for a run in the snow. He put on his parka and snow boots and left.

CHAPTER NINE

When the door closed behind Smitty, The Brick turned to Shannon and said, "I am real glad that you came to stay this week. I'm glad that you saw the mill, and that you saw the books so you can see how much the mill can make."

"And why are you so happy about all that?"

"Because," he said, as he got down on one knee, "I want to ask you to marry me, and I want you to see that I can support you. Will you marry me?"

"Yes, I love you and I would have married you anyway."

They talked on, as Smitty and Sherpa walked up the

road to the ford of the creek, the one thing that he most wanted to fix around here. He was thinking about using the backhoe from the mill to work on it when he noticed that the wind had picked up and it was starting to snow, just a few flakes at first, then more. He headed back. By the time he got back to the house it was almost a white out. If it kept up like this, he would have to plow the road twice a day just to keep up with it. At the house, Smitty tied up the dog, shook the snow off his hat and coat and went in. Shannon and the Brick came out of the kitchen all wrapped up in each other. Smitty asked, "How do you walk all tangled up like that?" The Brick ignored the wisecrack and blurted out the news. Smitty just nodded, "Well I'm glad that's over. I thought The Brick was going to explode waiting to ask you but I did think Shannon had more class than to say yes to a bum like you." Shannon reminded him, "He's your partner."

"Yeah, I guess that makes me a bum, too. Well, congratulations. I hope you have all the happiness in the world, but you still have to sleep in separate rooms."

The wind picked up during the night. By morning it was a blizzard. The trees nearest the house were barely visible through the blowing snow. It had snowed about two feet of new snow by then but the drifts were a lot deeper. Smitty got up early to check on the snow. As soon as he saw the conditions, he cranked up the truck and cleared the parking area. The Brick came out and helped put the chains on all four wheels. Smitty went back in the house to get a pistol, and a hand held CB radio. He called for Shannon to come downstairs, "Good morning, beautiful. We're going out to clear the road before it gets too deep to get through. I turned on the CB here, and have a hand held one to take with us. If we have a problem we will call you. I am leaving the dog here. He will tell you if the Boogy Man comes around. Shannon looked out the window and wondered, "Are you going to be able to find the road?"

"Yeah, I put up markers. We'll be back in about a half hour or so. See you then."

Some of the markers were buried in the drifts but they got the road cleared without too much trouble. Shannon had breakfast ready when they got back. As they came in and were getting out of their coats and snow boots, she scolded them, "I almost called you; you were gone a lot longer than 'or so'. Was it bad?" The Brick confessed, "Yes, I don't know how he found the road. The markers were on my side but I swear I only saw two of them. The snow was coming down so thick that you couldn't see much, and he was driving at about fifty. The snow flying off the blade was making it impossible to see a thing." Shannon just looked at

Smitty. He smiled. "You know how he exaggerates but the drifts were bad. I'll have to plow every four or five hours if it keeps snowing like this."

It was still acting like a blizzard at noon. After lunch they went out to plow again. This time Shannon and Sherpa went along. The snow wasn't as deep as it had been in the morning, so it went quicker. When they got back to the cabin Shannon told Smitty, "I couldn't see much out there. If it was worse this morning then I am going to have to agree with John. You must have a built in radar or something." Smitty said, "It wasn't too bad. I think we should turn on the radio and find out when this is going to let up."

"Can you pick up a radio station out here?" The Brick asked.

"No, but with the short wave set you can call all around the world. There are news and weather stations, too."

Smitty went to a cabinet in the front room, opened the door, and turned on the set. He turned the dial until he came to a news channel, then turned up the volume. The announcer was giving the world news about the Vietnam war, strife in Iran, then, "Now on the local news is a story of a small plane gone missing. It took off from the airport at Reno two days ago and has not been heard from since. The flight plan that the pilot filed was for San Francisco, which is only an hour and a half trip. The friends and family of the passengers are worried that they have been caught in the blizzard. The local Sheriff said today that they would start searching for the lost plane as soon as the weather cleared up some. The names of the people will be held until the relatives have been notified." Smitty got out a map of California, studied it and said, "If they took a direct route from Reno to Frisco, they would have flown right over us. That wind is blowing from the north. They could have been blown off course and gone down anywhere in the Eldorado National forest." The Brick agreed, "Or, the way that wind is blowing, they could be in Mexico."

The storm did not let up for four more days. The wind slowed down some but the snow kept coming. By the time it stopped, it was over six feet deep, and the berm beside the road was even higher. It was like driving down a tunnel. That night at dinner, Shannon said, "You know, with all that wind and heavy snow, I'm surprised that the power didn't go out." The Brick said, "Mr. Self-reliant here isn't hooked up to anything, no power, water, phone, or garbage pick-up. He has a wind generator for power; the water comes by gravity from a spring up the hill; he uses a radio instead of a phone, and the dog takes care of most of the garbage. Besides, if he had any monthly bills, he would have to work instead of roaming the woods and writing unpublished books." Smitty smiled. "I like the way you put it into words, Brick. It sounds like the ideal life. I'm glad no one listens to you, or the woods would soon be full of people looking for their Eldorado in the Eldorado." Shannon nodded, "It sounds pretty good to me, but I don't know about the loneliness. Why don't you find yourself a wife?"

"I like it here, and most women would not want to live with a poor cripple with no phone or TV. Women like all the modern conveniences." With that, he put on his hat and coat, went out and strapped on his snow shoes and climbed over the drifts and headed out for a walk in the woods with Sherpa padding along behind.

Shannon and the Brick got up from the table and watched him disappear into the woods. Shannon mused, "He's probably right about most women, but what's that about a poor cripple?"

The Brick, being the blunt kind of guy he is, blurted out, "He had half his leg blown off in Nam. The poor part is he doesn't get much on his disability. The good part is he gets around real good on his wooden leg, and he has things set up here so he can live without worrying about anything. Right now he is worried about that plane, though. He's sure it isn't far from here, and if they don't find it soon the people might freeze if anyone survived the crash, and didn't land in some cow pasture."

For the next few days, Smitty studied the forest service maps, and listened to the radio news station about the missing plane. It was time to take Shannon back to town. The Brick decided to stay in town with her; she would take him to the airport in a couple of days when he had to go back to the base. While in Reno, Smitty went to the Sheriff's office to check on the progress of the search. He told the receptionist that he lived in the back country, knew the wilderness area better than anyone, and would like to help with the search. One of the deputies took him into the search command room where he was introduced to the people running the search. He knew Frank Ward from the forest service. They had run into each other in the wilderness area once, and had stopped and talked for a while.

"Smitty," Mr. Ward said, "just the man we need." Smitty responded, "Good to see you, Frank. With you on the job those people are as good as found." Frank told the deputies, "This guy knows that area better than anybody." He queried Smitty, "We have had planes out from can see to can't see and haven't found anything yet. Have you any ideas?" Smitty went to the map. "I think they got caught in the blizzard. Their wings would have iced up pretty fast. I believe they would have been blown far to the south. Did you look in this area?" Frank said, "They must have gone down pretty early on in the storm and were probably buried. If there is anybody left alive, we haven't seen any movement or markers or anything. We don't believe they could have stayed up long enough to get blown that far south. So far we are concentrating our search in the northern part of the Eldorado but you could be right. We'll try farther south."

Smitty stayed with his dad for the next two days, spending a lot of time at the search command room checking on their progress. The rest of the time he spent buying dried food packages and other cold weather survival gear. He went to the airport to see The Brick off when it was time for him to go. The Brick pounded him on the back, shook his hand and said, "Thanks for letting me stay with you, old buddy. I can't wait until my time is up with Uncle Sam's misguided children, so I can come back and take up my duties as your partner and this beautiful lady's husband." Shannon said, "You see that I only rate second in all his plans." The Brick went into a long apology but Smitty cut him off with, "Save it for later. Kiss her goodbye or you will miss your plane."

"The Brick nudged him, "You are going after them, aren't you? That's why you stayed in town: to buy supplies." He grabbed Shannon, gave her a big kiss and took off for his plane. Shannon said, "I must be crazy to marry such a nut."

"He's a nut but he is the most loyal guy you'll ever meet. He will love you forever."

Ranger Ward was not surprised to see Smitty walk into the command center that afternoon, but he was a little surprised when Smitty said, "Well, I think I'll go look for them." One of the deputies proclaimed his opinion, "That's not a good idea. You go out there and then we'll be looking for you, too." Smitty countered, "In the Marines I went to cold weather training twice. I have cold weather gear, dried food, first aid stuff, a cargo sled, a St. Bernard, and snow shoes." Walking over to the map, he took one of the pins and stuck it in the map, "This is where my base camp will be. I'll be working the area around there. I'll call on the short wave when I get back." He wrote down the frequency to call them on and left.

Before the Deputy could say anything, the Ranger spoke, "Don't worry, he'll be okay. In fact, let's put some money on who finds them first." Since they were government employees, the wagers didn't get too high.

CHAPTER TEN

Back at the ranch, Smitty worked until way after dark packing and loading the sled for the trip. He had to make sure that he had everything that he might need, but he also had to keep it as light as possible. He wrote down everything on a check list as he loaded. The sky was still as black as the inside of a black cow when Smitty went out to feed Sherpa in the morning. He made himself a big breakfast; it would be late before he could eat again. As he ate, he went over the list to see if he had forgotten anything. He cleaned up the dishes, then went under the house, turned off the water, and opened the valves to drain the pipes so they wouldn't freeze while he was gone.

He put on his cold weather gear, locked up the cabin, put the harness on the dog, put on his snow shoes, and they were off into the gray dawn. The snow was deep and powdery. Smitty's pack was heavy and he was over two hundred pounds so even with his big snow shoes he still sank pretty deep. It was going to be a long day trudging through the deep snow but, with Smitty breaking trail, Sherpa wasn't having any trouble with the sled. The limbs on the trees were loaded down with snow, and every time he brushed one it would cause a small avalanche. The sun came up into a clear sky above a winter wonderland of unbelievable beauty. At this elevation the winter air was crystal clear and cold. Even though Smitty wore a ski mask breathing hard in the thin cold air hurt his lungs.

They stopped for a breather every couple of hours. The cold made his stump ache. It felt better when it was warm, and he was warmer when he was moving. He ate a granola bar for lunch, and gave one to the dog, too. By the time the sun was just above the mountains on the coast, they were on the edge of the area he wanted to search. They came out of the woods onto a ridge line that the wind had blown almost bare. The ridge went a long ways to the south, and the valleys on both sides were the first places he wanted to look. They made better time on the ridge, but it was getting dark pretty fast. They pulled off the top onto an old game trail and into a thick stand of firs where there was a small almost level spot for a camp. He unhooked the dog from the sled to let him do his duty while he set up camp.

After they had eaten, Smitty washed up the dishes in a pot of melted snow. He banked up the fire and he and the dog climbed into the tent where he rolled up in a blanket and went to sleep.

It was still pretty dark in the morning when they left camp for the ridge top again. They stopped every couple hundred yards so that Smitty could search the valley floor with his binoculars. After searching one side of the ridge, he would cross over and search the other side as best he could. The snow was deep enough on the valley floor to bury a small plane. The only way he would see anything was if someone was moving around outside the plane. If they were too banged up to get out, well, they would be dead soon anyway.

They moved along this way all day, with nothing to show for it. They were nearing the end of the long ridge, and the sun was almost to the mountains in the west. This was also where he had told Frank that he was going to make his base. The top of the ridge was no longer bare of trees.

It was necessary to back track to a clearing large enough to land a chopper. He stopped short of the clearing to set up camp in the protection of the trees. He turned Sherpa loose to run and dug out the markers to put out on the snow in the clearing. Smitty was worried. It was cold enough out here to freeze a polar bear's nose and the plane had been missing a long time. He cut some long stakes to hold the markers down and headed for the center of the clearing. Sherpa was sniffing around at the edge of the trees. Suddenly, Sherpa stopped short and listened, looking out towards the east.

Smitty wasn't watching. He went out to start laying out the black marker panels. He had just finished staking them out when he heard the dog start barking. His big woofs were coming from the east edge of the ridge. In the silence of the deep snow, it sounded loud enough to wake up some hibernating bears. Smitty headed through the woods towards the sound. As he came out of the trees he saw the dog standing on a large rock formation that jutted out from the edge of the ridge. Sherpa looked around quickly as Smitty walked up behind him then looked back down into the valley below and started woofing again. Smitty told him to shut up so he could listen. He heard a girl's voice calling for help. Well, it was either a girl or a very effeminate dude.

Smitty called down, "We're coming but it will take

a little time to find a way." It was after dark by the time they got down to the plane but with the girl calling and the dog woofing to guide them they made it. The plane was totally buried in the snow, and so close against the bottom of the cliff that you couldn't see it from the cliff top at all. It had plowed into the trees there at the base of the cliff after skidding across the valley floor.

A very pretty girl crawled out from under the wing wrapped in a blanket. "Mom thinks both of her legs are broken; she and I are the only ones left alive." She just stood there staring at Smitty as though she wasn't sure he was real. He smiled a little, "I'm Wayne Smith; they call me Smitty. The dog is Sherpa. I'll set up camp and get some soup on. You're probably hungry."

He moved off a ways from the plane and got set up as quickly as he could. First he dug down to the ground, set up the cook tent and stove and then the cold weather sleeping tent. He put the tent heater in it and lit it so it would be warm when he moved the women in. He put a pot of snow on to heat and filled the coffee pot full of snow to melt for coffee. He set up two low cots with sleeping bags in the sleeping tent.

Smitty then dug a better ramp down under the plane's wing to the door. He needed a gentle slope to carry the woman out. Even with the blizzard diet plan of not eating for a couple of weeks, it was still going to be difficult to get her out of the plane with two broken legs. When he was ready he opened the door to the plane; the girl climbed out. Smitty stuck his head into the plane to assess the situation. "Hi, I'm Wayne Smith, they call me Smitty." She was a beautiful woman in her late forties; she was in bad shape. She spoke very softly, "I'm Mary Mc Gregor and I'm very glad to see you. I'm afraid that you will have a very messy job ahead of you, Smitty."

Looking around he could see that he was going to have to move the bodies of the two men before he could get the lady out of the back seat. He told Mrs. McGregor that fact and she just nodded. He lifted the man nearest him out of the plane and set him in the snow. Then he unfastened the seatbelt of the pilot and dragged him across the plane. The seatbelt was stuck, either frozen to him or impaled on something. He ripped it loose, then lifted him out and set him in the snow next to the lady's husband. He folded the front seats down and climbed in and sat down next to the lady. If it wasn't so cold, the smell in there would have been unbearable. Even so, it was pretty bad. Mary had not been able to move out of her seat for over two weeks so her pants were pretty full. She could see by the look on Smitty's face exactly what he was thinking. "You have my permission to do whatever is needed to get me cleaned up, Smitty; did you bring a bath tub?"

"I brought a big wash tub, but I'm going to have to clean you up first before I can set you in it. I'll carry you to the tent and get things ready. Maybe your daughter can help." He then began to very carefully move her out of the plane. Somehow Smitty managed to get Mary out and through the door without banging her broken legs.

She smelled awful. He was not going to wash those clothes; he decided he would just chuck them. As he carried Mary into the cook tent, he told the daughter, "Lay that blanket you've got around you on the floor over there and help me with your mom."

"Who are you to give me orders, you pig. Do you know who you're talking to?"

"Yes, you are Sonja McGregor, who they call Sonny. It was all over the news. And I may be a pig but I don't smell as bad as you. Now put the blanket down?" He was thinking *you rich little brat.* Mary said, "Sonny, will you do as he says? I'm sure that he doesn't want to hold me like this forever." Sonny went to the spot Smitty had indicated, took the blanket from around her shoulders and spread it on the floor of the tent. Smitty very gently laid Mary down and turned her on her side. Smitty was nervous, "I haven't had any practice at this, Mary. I just hope that I don't hurt you too much getting you cleaned up."

"Don't worry, it will be so good to get clean that I can stand the pain, and I think you will be a lot more uncomfortable than I am."

"Come with me, Sonja. I need your help finding the right suitcase for some clean clothes for your mom."

Now let your imagination take you through the part about taking off her pants and cleaning her bottom. Suffice it to say it was painful for her and embarrassing for him. When finished, he threw a towel over her lower parts and went to work on setting her legs. He had never done this before either but had seen a lot of training films on it in the Marines. She did a lot of groaning, and they both did a lot of sweating but he got the bones back to where they seemed right to him. He put on the blow up splints that he brought with him. Smitty dumped the water off the stove into the wash tub, and a pot of snow in to cool it off, while Sonja helped her mom get the rest of her clothes off. With a very red face, he lifted the laughing, naked Mary into the tub. While Sonja washed her mom, Smitty went out to cut firewood.

The snow had buried the dry wood on the ground. He had to take a lantern with him to see anything. From a standing tree he cut some of the lower dead limbs that he could reach, and found a small, dead fir that he fell with his axe. He bucked it up with a bow saw, and carried a load in. Sonja met him at the entrance saying, "I can't lift mom out of the tub. Will you help?" He grabbed a couple of camp chairs off the sled and went in and lifted a naked, grinning Mary out of the tub and set her on one of the chairs. Mary teased, "Haven't you ever seen a naked woman before, Smitty?"

"Not such a lovely one, ever." Red faced, he left the tent in a hurry. He stacked a bunch of fire wood just outside the tent flap and took a box of food in and made supper. Sonja said, "I would like some roast turkey, mashed potatoes and gravy, and pie ala mode"

"Coming right up." While the soup was cooking he put together the fold up Alaska wood stove, and started a fire. He gave the two women a bowl of broth and a cup of tea, and explained, "You can have some broth every couple of hours for a few days, until your stomach will accept something solid."

"How long will it be before we can leave here?" Mary asked.

"If it doesn't snow, the forest service choppers should find us in a couple of days. I put out markers up on top of the ridge before I came down."

"And if it does?"

"I brought plenty of food, and when Sonja is strong enough to walk out of here we will load you on the sled and leave. It took us two days to get here from my place. It should take about the same going back."

"You must live way out in the woods. Do you work for the forest service?" Sonja asked.

"No. I am a writer, and a part owner of a saw mill. Now I need to turn in. I've had a long day." He carried Mary into the other tent and tucked her in. When she asked, "What about a toilet?" he said, "Yes, ma'am, I'll set one up right now."

It was earlier than he thought when he went to bed so he was wide awake long before daylight. He urgently needed to pee so he got dressed and went out. It was snowing big heavy flakes. If it didn't stop that meant no choppers today. He went out to the place he cut down the tree and carried in another load of wood and started a fire. He put a little water in the soup and set it on the wood stove to warm up. From the other tent he heard Mary call him. She needed to pee, too. He lifted her out of her bed and carried her to the fold up camp toilet set up in the corner of the cook tent. He held her while she got her pants down then set her on the toilet and got out from behind the blanket he had hung up for a curtain. Mary said from behind the blanket, "Are there no women in your family, Smitty?"

"No, my mom died. I just have a brother and a baby sister. Then I went in the Marines, and right after boot camp they sent us overseas. The only women I've been around were the nurses at the hospital when I got wounded, and they were officers."

Sonja appeared from the other tent. He had set up the tents so that the entrance to the sleeping tent was inside the back flaps of the cook tent. That way the heat from the wood stove would warm both tents. When Sonja stood straight up in the bigger tent, she was standing right in front of Smitty with less than a foot between them. He was six two; she was five eight. He could tell by the look on her face that she was mad about something. He should have figured, it being the sixties and the war still going on, she had to be an antiwar jerk. She took off with, "So you are one of those killers of women and children who are slaughterers of innocent people in a country where we have no business. You should be ashamed of yourself."

Before anyone could say anything more, Mary called from behind the screen, "Would you help me off the pot please, Smitty." He went in, picked her up and held her until she got her pants fixed, then he carried her out and set her on one of the chairs next to the card table. He said, "The soup is on the stove. I have to go up on the ridge and clean the snow off the markers so that the choppers will see them." He put on his parka and left.

CHAPTER ELEVEN

Smitty put on his snow-shoes and headed up the path to the ridge. Back in the tent, Sonja started to say something more but Mary put her finger to her lips, "Would you get me a bowl of the broth, please?" Sonja glared at her for a moment, then turned and did as she was told. She handed the bowl to her mom, who instructed her, "Get yourself one, too, and sit down. It's time we had a mother daughter chat." Sonja got herself a bowl of broth and sat across from her mom. Mary looked at her daughter and began, "I think that your dad and I were remiss in teaching you proper manners. Our Mr. Smith does not work for the government. He came to rescue us all on his own. He bought all the gear and food and came looking for us in the middle of a blizzard. It is time for you to grow up and stop trying to act like some antiwar hippie. After the way you just treated Smitty, I wouldn't blame him if he just left us here. So let me tell you something: if he decides to leave I will talk him into taking me with him and you will be left here alone. I hope the bears don't get you before I can get a rescue team to come back for you."

"Mother, you have never spoken to me like this before." Mary glared at her daughter but with a lot of love in her heart. "It's time you started treating people better. You think you are better than everyone because you are rich. Well, my daughter, you are not rich. I am. Without Smitty we may never have been found. We would have been dead soon. Right now he is the most important person in the world to us and you had better start treating him like he is. I mean it. If you don't clean up your act right now, when we get back I am going to cut off all your money. No car. No allowance. I will only buy your new clothes at the Good Will. Now will you please get me another bowl of soup? And then you had better have an attitude change. I don't want you to speak to Smitty until you do."

It was snowing again, big heavy flakes. It was not

going to do any good, uncovering the markers. They would be recovered before he could walk back down the hill. Smitty didn't notice the snow or the steepness of the trail. His mind was on what that spoiled brat Sonja had said. In his opinion she was of the age group that was against the war because they were cowards. He thought about what a weak place this would be when they were the adults of this country, which wasn't very far off. He realized that he would have no trouble ignoring her and everything she said if she wasn't so damn pretty. A warning light blinked in his head. No, he couldn't be falling for this little snot. Nothing could come of it. Here he was a one legged unpublished mountain man writer, and she was a whatever she was. I can't imagine her being happy at my cabin, or me being happy in her mom's mansion. So he instructed himself to put it out of his mind and start planning how to get them out of here.

Coming back down the hill, Smitty saw that the snow was causing the tent tops to sag precariously. He spent the rest of the day building a shelter of poles and tree limbs over the tents to keep the snow off. After feeding the dog he went to the food cache in the trees and brought in some packs. "I'm making chicken noodle soup tonight and in the morning we'll have pancakes." Mary asked, "Could you help me to the potty first? You have been gone a long time."

A few days later Smitty announced, "You girls have been eating pretty well lately. I think it's time to see how Sonja does on snow-shoes." Sonja started to say something, but her mother cut her off. "I think you are right, Smitty. We surely need to leave before the food runs out. I'm sure you and Sherpa can't pull both of us out of here." Smitty handed his pistol to Mary and asked, "Just in case some lonely critter comes to visit, do you know how to use it?"

"Yes, I am a very good shot. Do you think I will need it?"

"No, if I did I wouldn't leave. We won't go far but in your condition you would be completely helpless if you did have a visitor. Sonja, dress warm. It's snowing pretty hard and it's very cold out."

"Yes sir," she said, giving him a military salute before going into the sleeping tent to put on more clothes. She came out dressed in her ski clothes, hat, and gloves. Smitty showed her how to lace on her snow-shoes and they took off across the valley with the dog walking behind. He was too smart to go out ahead; he walked where the snow is mostly packed by the people on snow shoes. Crunching through the snow Smitty kept looking back; when he couldn't see the camp anymore he turned in a big circle and headed back to the woods where he had been cutting fire wood. Sonja, panting to keep up said, "If a person was in shape, this could be fun. The air is so crisp and clean and the country so beautiful that if you didn't walk so fast it would be enjoyable."

"We need to get your legs in shape. It's about a twelve hour walk out of here, mostly uphill. I would like to make it in one day so we don't have to carry a lot of camp gear with us. It would make the trip twice as long and twice as hard on your mom." She thought to herself, *"Me? Walk on snowshoes for twelve hours straight? No way. I couldn't do it. Even two six hour walks would be too much."* She didn't say anything, though. She didn't want Smitty saying anything mean like she was a lazy spoiled brat kid or something. She didn't want to admit it but she was beginning to like the big quiet man. He did everything well. He was very much the gentleman. He could have taken advantage of her and her mom. He didn't even ask for money. Wow! She was really making a white knight out of the guy. If she wasn't careful she just might fall in love with him. She decided to work hard on getting in shape so she could get out of here and away from this big klutz. The thought of big dumb looking Smitty out with her friends was pretty funny. She could imagine one of her friends asking him, "How many times did you bang Sonja and her mom while you had them under your power?" She wondered what he would say or more likely what he would do to them. He would probably kill the guy being as he was one of those murderers from the Marines. He seemed so gentle, though. It just didn't seem possible that he could be a murderer. He's strong enough to break someone in half. Look at him up there breaking trail; that's hard work and he isn't even breathing hard.

When they arrived at the wood pile, Smitty loaded up a big arm load of the split wood and headed for the tents. Sonja loaded up what she could and went after him. Instead of the smart remark she expected he said, "Thank you for helping with the wood. You did well on the snow-shoes, too. You should be strong enough in just a few days.

The snow-shoe trips got longer and longer. The talks between them also got longer. Once she was going to say something about the war but she decided to ask a few questions instead. What he told her was a bit of a shock: a short rundown on the good things that they had done for the people and that he had never shot at anybody because he was a radio operator. He told her of growing up on the farm and of getting football scholarships for college. During the summer between his second and third year he got a draft notice. He decided to get it over with and joined the Marines.

"Why didn't you go back and finish your schooling?"

"Because I got wounded over there and I wouldn't be

able to get any more scholarships." She didn't know that she was about to touch a nerve but she did. "You don't seem to be handicapped so why couldn't you go back?" He didn't answer her; he just kept walking. His silence irritated her and it was evident in her voice, "Is it a military secret or something?" He answered in a low but sharp tone, "They don't let one legged men play football." This shocked her into silence for the rest of the walk.

When they got to the tent Smitty picked up the small radio and headed up the hill with the dog trailing along. Sonja unlaced her snow-shoes and went in. She put wood in the stove and put some soup on to boil. She had been thinking about what Smitty said. She turned to her mom, "Mom, did you know that Smitty has a prosthesis?"

"I suspected something like that. While he was carrying me around I put my hand on his leg and felt some kind of brace. He knew that I felt it and didn't say anything so I didn't either."

"You wouldn't know there was anything wrong with him."

"There isn't. He either doesn't think about it or is ashamed of it so he doesn't talk about it. It doesn't slow him down any. Where is he? I need to go potty."

"He went up the hill with the radio. He was mad at me

for asking about his wounds."

Smitty, upon reaching the top, pulled the markers out from under the snow and reset them. It was still snowing, but not as hard. He got out the radio and called in. On the third try he got a little crackle but that was all. He decided to send a message anyway just in case they could hear him. "Base, this is Smitty. I found them. The pilot and Mr. McGregor are dead but the women are okay. Mrs. McGregor has two broken legs but I set them in splints and she is fine. We are leaving in the morning from the base camp that I marked on your map. We are running low on food and can't wait any longer. Smitty out." There was a lot of crackling on the radio, which was a good sign. It meant they may have heard some of it anyway. When it stopped, he said, "I am not receiving you and will proceed as planned. If you got any of this meet us along the way to my place with four Big Macs. Sherpa loves them. Smitty out."

Then he hurried down the hill to tell the girls that he might have gotten through to the search party and that help may be on the way. Mary cheered, "That's great, Smitty. Are we going to wait here for them to come get us?"

"No, we will take off in the morning and meet them half way if they heard me. If not, we will be at my house tomorrow night and I can call them from there." While the women talked about what they were going to wear, Smitty packed for the trip. He was glad there was no more talk about his peg leg.

CHAPTER TWELVE

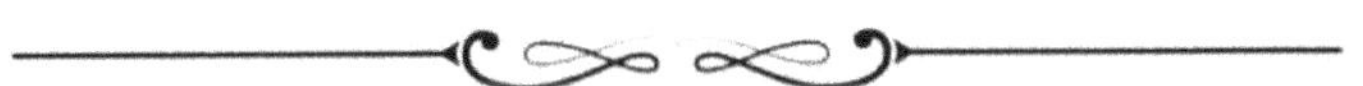

Smitty was up early in the morning loading the sled. He only took what he thought they might need and nothing extra: a couple of tarps to make a shelter, the sleeping bags, what food they had left, a small axe, and the bow saw, just in case they had to spend the night on the trail. He got the women up, dressed in warm clothes, and fed. He laid out his and Sonja's sleeping bags on the sled with the rest of the load piled in the middle, so that Mary could sit up and lean back against the tied down load. He went back into the tent and told Mary, "Okay, I am going to put you back in your sleeping bag before I load you on the sled with the rest of the stuff." She laughed and said, "Like a sack of potatoes, huh? What about the tents and stoves and the rest of your gear, Smitty?"

"I'll come back and pick it up later." He almost said when we pick up the bodies but decided that might be a little insensitive. They got into their snow-shoes and put the harness on Sherpa. Smitty instructed Sonja, "Take the rope tied to the back of the sled and try to keep the sled from sliding sideways off the trail and down over the side of the hill. Getting up this steep trail to the top is going to be the hardest part of the trip. Okay?"

Yes, Mr. Smith. I will do exactly as I'm told, Mr. Smith." Mary spoke through the muffler around her face, "Sonja, I am warning you."

"I was just kidding, Mom. It's cool."

"It sure is."

Smitty asked Mary, "Are you warm enough? It is pretty cold out here."

"Oh, it's toasty under here. I don't think I'll get cold with all these blankets on me. Let's go." Smitty picked up the lead rope, put the loop over his head and around his ribs and headed up the trail.

It was a struggle going up that steep trail, but the sled moved along easily with the light load that was on it. It was fairly level on the top of the ridge and they moved out at a pretty good rate of speed. Two hours later, as it was getting light, Mary called, "Smitty, wait." He stopped and turned to see what was wrong. "Listen. I thought I heard a motor of some kind."

"Yeah, it sounds like a bunch of snowmobiles. I couldn't hear over the crunch of snow shoes." He took out the radio and turned it on. He hung it on the front of his parka, then started on. About half an hour late it came to life. "Smitty, this is rescue one. Can you hear me?" Smitty stopped, grabbed the radio and responded, "Rescue one, this is Smitty. I can hear you loud and clear and it's good to hear your voice. Over."

"Smitty, it's good to hear you, too. We got your message the other time and headed out early this morning to meet you. Oh yeah, we brought the hamburgers, too." Smitty walked back to the sled, and Sonja walked up beside him so they could all hear the radio. "Where are you now, Smitty?"

"If you are heading for my base camp, we will meet you along the way. We could hear a lot of noisy snowmobiles earlier. If that is you just keep on and we will see you in a little while. Smitty out." Sonja, with tears running down her face, said, "We are going to be saved." To which Mary responded, "We were saved when we heard Sherpa barking that first night. We would have reached his place tonight. You have done a wonderful job of it, Smitty, and all by yourself. When people talk of heroic deeds, your name is going to be at the top of the list. You will always be my hero, Smitty, and I will always consider you my best friend." Sonja threw her arms around him and said, "Me too, Smitty. I love you, and not just for what you've done. You are not only a great guy; you are my hero, too." It hit Smitty that he was in love with her, too, but he figured that her love for him would wear off when she got back with her friends. "I love you two, too. It has been a real adventure. I think I'll write a book about it. If you don't mind me taking a little literary license with it, it should be a pretty good story."

They took off again. The snow had stopped and the view from the top of the ridge was great. The snow covering the trees, ridges, and valleys on both sides of them was nature at its most beautiful. They could hear the snow machines getting closer. Mary called from the sled, "Would you mind if we stayed at your place for a while, Smitty, just until we get everything settled up here? I mean if you have room." He didn't stop going. He just yelled over his shoulder, "You can stay forever if you want. I'm your friend, remember? When my dad sees how pretty you are he is going to want to come stay, too."

"Does he live close?"

"He lives in Reno. He sold the farm and moved up here when I did."

Forty minutes later the snowmobiles came out of the trees up ahead. They were soon surrounded by men on sleds all jabbering at once and pounding Smitty on the back and asking the women how they were. Frank Ward took Smitty aside and asked, "Will it be hard to find the crash site?"

"No, just back trail us. You should be there shortly. It's only about twelve miles or so. The bodies are under the plane wing. Would you bring back the rest of my gear? It's all stacked in the tents."

"No problem, Smitty. Listen, the Sheriff leaked the story that you found them to the press. You know, when you go out and rescue the rich and famous, it's big news."

"Yeah, I think Mrs. McGregor is going to have a big solid gold hero badge made for me."

"Well, you deserve it, Smitty. We would probably never have found them. Here, you take the machine with no sled behind it. Just hook your cargo sled on behind and head for home. I will radio our base and have them send an ambulance to meet you at your place. They will want to check the women out, don't you think?"

They were soon on their way with Sherpa on the back of the sled and Sonja on the snowmobile behind Smitty. They took their time because the cargo sled wasn't meant to be pulled by a snowmobile. It still took less than three hours to get home. The ambulance was waiting at the house. So was Mr. Smith. He had been there a while. The lights were on, the water was once again running and smoke was coming from the chimney.

Smitty yelled out as he pulled up, "Hello, Dad. This is Mrs. McGregor, and her daughter Sonja." Mary reached out from under the blankets and shook his hand. "I am very glad to meet you, Mr. Smith. Smitty has told us nice things about you. I hope to get to know you. Did you know that your son is a real live hero?"

"Yes, I did know. He was decorated in the Marines for heroism and once a hero always a hero. I'm glad to see that he got you out. The press is going to be all over you when you get to town. I had to sneak away to get out here without being followed."

Smitty unwrapped Mary and carried her into the house to use the bathroom. When she was done, he went in and helped her get dressed and brought her out and laid her on the stretcher. She asked them, "When you two get cleaned up, would you come get me?" Mr. Smith interjected, "No,

I'll follow them in and bring her back, but it will probably be in the morning." Sonja said, "No fooling around, you two."

"You either," her mom responded.

Soon everyone was gone and it was just the two of them. Sonja said, "I am really looking forward to a nice hot shower which reminds me that I didn't bring any clothes with me from the plane. I guess I will just have to run around naked." Smitty blushed but he smiled at the thought. "The search party will bring your stuff back. In the meantime, I'll get you something to wear. You don't want one of those deputies to arrest you for indecent exposure."

"How do you know it would be indecent? You might like it."

"I'm sure I would. You are a very beautiful woman. A little smelly though, so go take a bath."

While Sonja bathed, Smitty made dinner. He fried some steaks and some potatoes then steamed some broccoli. Sonja came clomping out in a pair of his slippers, and a bathrobe, with her hair wrapped in a towel. She sat at the table. "Oh, Smitty, whatever you are making smells really good."

"I didn't make any for you. It's just peasant food."

"Tonight I'm a peasant. If you didn't make any for me, I will eat yours and you can eat dog food." He dished up the food, poured the coffee, and sat down. She waited for him with her hands folded in her lap until he started to cut his steak, then said, "Aren't you forgetting to pray? You always pray over your food, and tonight I think you should add a little something about getting us out of there." So he did.

When they had finished dinner, Sonja did the dishes and Smitty took a shower. They were sitting by the wood stove talking when they heard the snowmobiles coming. Smitty said, "I better go tie the dog up so he doesn't eat anybody. There will be a lot of stuff to unload, too, so I will be out a while. I will bring in your suit cases as soon as we get to them."

"Mine are the red ones. Bring them first, please."

By the time the snow machines got there, Smitty had shoveled a path wide enough for them to come down into the parking area. The snow was almost eight feet deep and that's a heck of a drop. It looked like they had backed the trucks right up to the snow bank to unload them. Smitty found the red suitcases and took them into the house. Sonja asked, "What about Dad?"

"They will take them to the morgue. You and your mom can see to that later."

When they were all unloaded and had loaded their sleds on the trucks, Frank said, "Well, you did a good job,

Smitty. That camp looked like you could have stayed the winter with no problem and with two beautiful women to keep you warm. Not too shabby."

"Yeah, but we were about to get hungry. I hauled in too much comfort and not enough food."

"I made some money, betting that you would find them before we did. I'm sure we'll be asking for your help in the future."

It was late by the time everybody left. Sonja was asleep on the couch. She woke up when he opened the wood stove door to stoke it up before going to bed. She begged, "Carry me to bed, Smitty. I didn't know which one to sleep in." He picked her up and started for the stairs but she continued, "Can I sleep with you? I promise not to rape you."

"I don't think I can promise that."

"I don't care. I think I love you, Smitty." He headed for his room, saying, "I love you, too."

The morning came with a clear sky and the look of a winter wonderland outside. The air was so cold that Sherpa's breath was making frost on his whiskers. He didn't care; he liked the cold. He thought it was getting late and he wanted his breakfast so he woofed a few times to see if that would hurry things along. It worked. In a few minutes Smitty came out with his food; that man and that dog did have a great love for each other. Smitty looked around at the beauty of the winter decorated forest. He loved it out here in the woods. The fact that he and Sonja had made promises of eternal devotion to each other last night made him a little uneasy. He was pretty sure that Sonja would not want to live the isolated life that he lived and he was real sure that he could not stand to live in the bay area. Oh well, they would have to work something out. He went in and started breakfast.

It was four in the afternoon when Mr. Smith brought Mary back. She came in on crutches, wearing an old bathrobe. She said, "I am freezing my rear end off. Let me sit by the stove. I haven't anything on under this robe. I had to get out of that hospital. The media were driving me crazy so I couldn't send Don to buy me something to wear. I hope my suitcases are here."

"Yes ma'am, I put them in the downstairs bedroom. It has its own bathroom and no stairs to climb." Don said, "You should have heard the speech she made to the media. I swear, if you don't get a congressional medal of honor I will be surprised."

"Well, he deserves one. Sonja, show me to my bedroom and help me get some clothes on. I'm a little cold down under."

That evening, as they were all sitting around talking,

Mary took the floor, "We have a few things that we need to talk over. The first is, I am the sole owner of a large manufacturing company and I have had very little to do with running it. I am going to need some help. Smitty, did she molest you last night?" He turned beet red. Sonja said, "Yes I did, and I don't plan to quit either."

"Has he asked you to marry him?"

"No, but he will." Smitty stayed red and uncomfortable. His dad and Mary both laughed. Smitty squirmed, "I was going to ask her, but I didn't have any real hope that she would accept."

"Why?"

"Because she is rich and beautiful and I'm a poor, ugly cripple." Mary laughed, "She is not rich. I am. And if you come help run our company I will make you president and pay you a fat salary. The ugly part we can't do much about, but you can throw the cripple stuff out the window. There isn't a man on this planet with two good legs that could have done what you did to save us any better than you did. Now will you come help me?"

Smitty just stared at the floor. He was thinking, I don't want to live in the city, but I would be near Sonja and if she meant that about not quitting the sex, it would be great. He raised his eyes to Mary's and replied, "Yes, I will. I have some obligations here though. ”

"If you mean your saw mill, I paid it off, and also I paid your dad the money that you owed him, although he probably raised the amount some but don't worry about it; just call it a reward for rescuing us.

"I didn't ask for a reward. I guess I could pay you back from the salary you pay me."

"No you won't." Sonja said, "When we get married, I will help you spend everything she pays you."

CHAPTER THIRTEEN

The story could end here, but then you would miss the true love conquers all part. A lot happened in the next two weeks. Smitty hired a contractor to build a bridge across the creek in the spring. He called The Brick and told him the whole story; he told him he would come up and help him build his house when he was ready but he would have to wait for spring anyway. In the meantime, he and Shannon could stay at his cabin. Now he was on his way to the Bay Area in the new Jeep that Mary bought him, with Sherpa in the back. He had one of those screens put in so Sherpa couldn't stick his head over the seats and slobber all over them. He was a little excited about going. He had never ever been in a big mansion with servants and a cook and all. The idea of eating all that good food that he didn't have to cook himself was making his mouth water. His dad said he would help The Brick at the mill when he needed him and that he would help on the house, too. His mind kept going back to that night that he had spent with Sonja and now he was going to live in the same house with her. She had said that they would get married, but he still couldn't believe it. He knew that he wouldn't fit in with her friends. The fact that he was a farm hick was bad enough but that he was an ex-marine was the real killer. In these anti- war times they lived in he would be an outcast for sure. He had doubts about his abilities running a big business, too. Well, he had to think positive. Someone was running it now. All he had to do was be the muscle behind Mary. He could be muscle all right.

Being the middle of the week, the traffic on highway 50W was light. Cruising along in his new Jeep was pure joy. He was enjoying himself and decided that even if things in the Bay Area didn't work out, he was a lot better off now than he had been before the rescue. His debts were paid off and he had a new car. All the money that the mill made they got to keep. And he did have that one night with Sonja to remember. All in all: not too bad.

Following the directions that Mary had given him he eventually drove up the driveway to the mansion. It was even bigger than he had imagined. He pulled up behind two other cars parked on the side of the driveway. It was almost noon; maybe they had guests for lunch. When he rang the bell, an old man dressed in evening clothes answered the door. "Hello, I'm Wayne Smith. I believe I'm expected." The old man bowed, "Please come in, Mr. Smith. The family has just been called for lunch. I will announce you if you will follow me." They walked down a long, wide hall past a lot of doors until the butler finally stopped, opened a door, stepped in and announced in a loud voice, "A Mr. Smith to see you, Madam." Smitty walked in and Sonja jumped up from the table and ran to meet him. She threw her arms around him and sang in an excited voice, "Here he is everybody. Our savior." She then gave him a big sloppy kiss and turned and introduced him around the table. The first thing he noticed was that the men were all in suits. He was wearing only slacks and a sweater. At least he had changed from snow boots to loafers, and had left his parka in the car. Later, he couldn't remember how many people were around the table or who they were. It seemed like there were at least nine or ten, though. Only a few were women but all were department heads of the company, so he would get to know them later. After lunch was finished and the rescue story had been told again by Sonja, Mary asked Smitty to tell how he had found them. He said, "That was easy. I just headed down wind until the dog smelled something and started barking."

"What did it smell?" someone asked.

"Well, Sonja was out wandering around and she hadn't had a bath in two weeks. Dogs have sensitive noses, you know." Sonja didn't think it was very funny. Smitty then told the whole story up until the time they met Sherpa. They all wanted to meet Sherpa; he was the real hero. After they finished eating they all trooped out to the driveway to see him. When Smitty opened the back of the Jeep Sherpa jumped out, ran a few steps and stopped to leave a large deposit in the middle of the road. The embarrassed Smitty said, "You'll have to excuse him, folks; he is just a country boy and it was a long trip."

Sonja took him around back and showed Smitty where to tie the dog up. While they were alone she told him, "We have planned a welcome party for you for Friday night here at the house. We want our friends to meet you. Is that all right?" He took her hand in his and asked, "Are you sure about all this, Sonja? Do you really love me?"

"Yes. Why? Do you think it's something else?"

"I don't know. You are so beautiful and I'm just a big ugly farm boy. I'm afraid you are just grateful for the rescue, and down the road you will break my heart."

"Oh Smitty, there is no one that I could love more and not just for the rescue but just because you're you."

"Then will you marry me? I haven't bought a ring but then I haven't been paid yet."

"Yes, I will marry you. Let's go downtown right now and I will help you pick one out. We will use mom's charge cards. Besides, you need some suits to work in. Okay?" She talked so fast that he didn't have time to argue. So, off they went.

The ring that they bought on Mary's charge card was a big one, of course. After all, Sonja helped pick it out. They bought four nice uptown looking suits with a dozen shirts with ties to match. He rebelled, but she said, "You have to wear them all the time and you can't wear the same one every day. Besides, you look so handsome all dressed up. Well, almost handsome." She made him get two pair of dress shoes, and a pair of tennis shoes, too.

"Why tennis shoes?"

"We have a tennis court in the back yard. You said you were good once. I want to see if you were lying. I'm the best tennis player of my friends and family; I need someone good to play with."

"You just want to see me make a fool of myself, running around in tennis shorts with a peg leg."

"That does sound funny but you don't have to wear shorts. When you see me in my skimpy little tennis outfit you probably won't last a whole set without wanting to stop for some other type of recreation anyway."

"You mean like a swim?"

"Yeah, to cool you off."

The next morning, all dressed up in a new suit, Smitty and Mary were driven to the plant in her Lincoln. She said, "Tomorrow is Friday, so today and tomorrow you will get to know your way around the plant. I won't expect you to take over the running of it until Monday."

"Oh yeah, that should be plenty of time. You will have someone show me around for the first hour or so, won't you?"

"If I have to. I will tell all the department heads that you are second in command and that whatever you say goes. I know that might put a little pressure on you but you're a big boy. Just take notes and we'll discuss any changes you think are needed before we make them. I haven't been doing this very long either. The man named Perkins who you met at lunch yesterday thinks he should be running the place, but

I don't trust him."

"We should be all right once we get it all figured out. How much did you have to do with it before?"

"I worked here as his secretary when we first started it but we were having so much fun with him chasing me around the desk that we decided that he should get a younger one who could outrun him better than I could. Since the secretary usually knows more about the business than the boss, I'm not completely in the dark but don't worry about it. You will be fine."

The limo pulled up in front of a large and very impressive manufacturing building and they went in. He had never felt more out of place in his life. As soon as they were in the office Mary called a staff meeting. When everyone was seated around the big table with a note pad and a cup of coffee, Mary started the meeting by saying, "This is Wayne Smith who most of you met at lunch yesterday.   He has been made vice president of the company. If you have any objections write it on your pad then file it in the round file." Nobody laughed. They all just stared at Smitty. She went on, "Mr. Warner, since you are head of personnel, you will get someone to show Mr. Smith around for the next few days and take him to the secretarial pool to have him pick out a secretary. She better not be too pretty or my daughter will make a fuss." A few people smiled this time. Mary got down to business then; Smitty listened. He needed to learn as much as he could as fast as he could. After the meeting, Mr. Warner, a busy little fat man, took Smitty in tow. He walked very fast down the hall to a room full of desks. When they walked in three women who had been chatting got busy all of a sudden. One of the others, a lady probably in her mid-thirties who had been typing very fast, glanced up. Smitty thought she was probably the best one. Mr. Warner announced in his nasal voice, "Attention everyone, this is Mr. Smith. He is our new vice president and he needs a secretary." He stepped aside and Smitty walked over to the one he had liked and said, "Would you like the job? It won't be easy because you will have to train me and I'm a slow learner." Her name plate said she was Sandra Mapes. She smiled a little and said in a little girl voice, "Yes, Sir." She looked down at her typewriter then back up at Smitty and asked, "May I finish this? It's important." Smitty looked at Mr. Warner and nodded. Warner said to Mrs. Mapes, "We will be in the old manager's office. How long will you be?"

"Ten minutes."

Mr. Warner led the way to Smitty's new office. *Mr. Wayne Smith* was already painted on the door. Smitty walked in, looked around and thought it was kind of small, but nice.

Mr. Warner walked past him, opened another door and said, "This way, please." Smitty walked into a much nicer and larger office. It even had a couch and some upholstered chairs around a coffee table. Mr. Warners said, "That will be Mrs. Mapes' desk out there. By the way, you picked the best one of the girls. She never flirts; she is strictly business. She is married to a big truck driver and is happy with that. Would you like me to show you around the plant now, or would you like to get settled in first?"

"I'm sure you have plenty to do. I will get Mrs. Mapes to show me around. Anyway, we need to get to know each other." Mr. Warner just nodded and left. Smitty tried out all the chairs then noticed another door; he opened it. It was a half bath so he tried that out, too. Since he was the only one there he didn't bother to close the door. Mrs. Mapes entered the office; she ignored him and started arranging things on her desk. When he finished he sat at his desk, and she came in. He told her to sit in one of the chairs, took out a small notebook from his desk and said, "I am going to need a lot of help. How much do you know about me?"

"The rumor is that you saved Mrs. McGregor and her daughter from a plane crash, kept them alive, got them out of the mountains all by yourself and they are understandably grateful."

"And that's why I got this job. Yes, that's the way I see it, too. Mrs. McGregor says that she needs help running this place. Do you believe that?"

"Yes." Then she looked a little worried.

"Look, you have to tell it like you see it. Whatever you say is just between us . I need to know what's going on around here if I'm going to help her. Okay?"

"Yes, sir. Some of the men here think that they should be running things."

"Yes, she mentioned someone named Perkins. What's his job?"

"He is in charge of sales and shipping. He is a bit pushy, but then he is a salesman."

Mrs. Mapes walked with Smitty all over the plant, introducing him to the people they met and explaining who he was. At lunch time the loud speaker commanded, "Mr. Smith, please report to Mrs. McGregor's office." When they got there he told Mrs. Mapes that he would see her after lunch and went in. Mary's secretary just pointed to a door and nodded. Smitty knocked and when he heard a response, walked in. Sonja stood in the middle of the room, all dressed up and posing like a model. "It's a new dress," she said, "What do you think?" The dress was a pale green with some of that see through stuff of the same color over the top. With her long wavy auburn hair worn down she was a knockout. He said, "It's very pretty, but on you anything would look great." She smiled very nicely with a lot of love in her eyes. Mary said, "She wants you to take her to lunch. When you get back come back here, we have some things to discuss. And take your time at lunch as I really don't expect much out of you until after you're married."

"Tell your daughter to let me work."

"It wouldn't do any good; she won't listen to me anymore." They had lunch on Fisherman's Wharf and walked along the docks looking at the boats and talking about the wedding. It reminded Smitty of the old saying that weddings are for women. He said, "Honey, you do all the planning. Just tell me when to show up and what to wear. I have enough on my mind with this new job. This is a whole new world to me." She was a little hurt.

"Okay. I guess if I have to do all the planning you won't mind if you and your men are wearing pink sports coats and shocking pink ruffled shirts with ties to match."

"Oh yes, I can just imagine what The Brick would say. I hope that none of your friends say anything anti-war where he can hear it. The whole thing could turn into a battle. And no, we cannot get married without him. He is just about my only friend."

"I wouldn't think of leaving him out; I am sure I will like him, too. I guess the new job would be a little overwhelming. I do need a list of people you want to invite, and their addresses."

When they got back to the office, he asked her, "How come you're driving my Jeep instead of your car?"

"It makes me feel like we are already married."

He kissed Sonja goodbye, and headed for Mary's office. All the way there, he was thinking about Sonja and worried about whether things were going to work out both here at the plant and with her. When he walked into the outer office he remembered the secretary's name and said, "Good afternoon, Joan. Is the boss in?"

"Yes, and I'm sure she will be glad to see you but duck when you open the door. It sounds as if they are about to start throwing things." During a loud outbreak in the talk he opened the door quietly and slipped in. Mary saw him, but not wanting anyone to notice he was there she kept her eyes on the two men standing in front of her desk. Mr. Perkins was saying, "I have told Mr. Parks that we need to buy Japanese parts to save money, but he won't do it. He gives me that Buy American crap and refuses. I want him replaced with someone more in tune with the times." Mary smiled, "I think for the time being we will continue as we are. I think Mr. Parks is doing a good job and unless he wants a change, will stay at it." Mr. Parks started to answer, but Mr. Perkins butted in saying, "I would like to remind you that I own a large block of stock in this company and at the next stockholder's meeting I am going to have a great deal to say."

During this little speech, Smitty walked up behind Mr. Perkins. Mary said, "Sit down, Mr. Perkins. Mr. Parks, would you excuse us? We have a few things to discuss and you probably have more important things to do than to listen to us." Mr. Parks, a husky Korean War vet, who was not easily ruffled, just nodded and left. When Mr. Perkins turned to watch him leave, he noticed Smitty standing behind him. He stepped quickly away. Smitty said, "Mary asked you to sit down; please do it." Mr. Perkins sat down, quickly. Smitty took another chair and Mary began, "I know that you own a great deal of stock, but 51 percent is under my control so it will not do you any good to go to the stock holder's meeting and try to vote me out because it won't work. Now, I have found that you made the phone call that brought us hurrying back from our trip, and caused the crash that killed my husband, the pilot, and if it hadn't been for Smitty, would have killed my daughter and me, too. What was so important that it couldn't wait until the weather cleared so we could get home safely?"

Mr. Perkins sat looking from his hands to Mary to Smitty and back at his hands again for a full minute, then said, "I told him that I had enough votes to take over the company and to come back now or just stay on vacation." Mary sat staring at him for a while then leaned forward, put her elbows on the desk and said, "So you waited until there was a blizzard coming before you called. I'll bet that you were elated when our plane was reported missing. So you were all ready to move into this office as soon as they gave up the search. I don't want to hear any more out of you. Get out. Oh, and by the way, you are fired." He jumped to his feet, leaned on the desk and shouted, "You may have the authority to fire me now, but I am calling a stockholder's meeting and we will vote you and your future son-in-law out into the street." Smitty stood and took him by the arm. As he was walking him to the door, he quietly instructed him, "Mary told you to get out. As you seem unable to do that on your own, I will assist you." He walked the sputtering Mr. Perkins out through the secretary's office and as he pushed him into the hall, instructed him, "Empty out the stuff from your office and leave the building."

When he returned, Mary was on the phone to security. "Go up and make sure he just takes his personal things and get his keys and passes. Keep those things at your desk. Mr. Smith will pick them up on his way out tonight. Thank you." As she hung up the phone Smitty asked, "Am I going to be out in the street on my first day or is the stockholder's meeting not until this weekend?" She laughed, "You're safe. When the word got out that the plane had gone down with all hands, our stock took a dive and someone put a good size chunk on the block. Since we have been trying to buy up our stock, we had a standing order with our broker to buy up anything that came up for sale and, although we didn't get it all, we got enough to take us over the fifty one percent mark. By the way, I had it put in your name, and you owe about forty thousand to the broker."

"Wow, first day on the job and I'm in debt forty thousand."

Back in his office, Smitty had some other thoughts. As instructed, he pushed a button on his intercom and his secretary entered. "Mrs. Mapes, Mary just fired Mr. Perkins. Will there be any problems in the finance department? Or does he have anything to do with that?"

"Not usually, but while everybody was gone he thought he owned the place so he might have. I'll check around. By the way, everyone calls me Sandy."

"Okay, everyone calls me Smitty and starting this

minute we are friends.   By the way, are you coming to the party Friday night?"

"We were not invited." she said, teasingly.

"You are now. It's formal. I need at least one friend there."

"Okay, but we will feel really out of place."

"Not any more than I do here."

Smitty noticed a large pile of papers on his desk. He picked them up and headed for Mary's office, said hello to Joan on his way through and walked in. Mary looked up as he walked in, "You should knock. I could have been having sex with a foreman."

"Now I'll never knock; that would be worth seeing. Now what am I supposed to do with this?" he asked, holding out the pile of papers.

"Why didn't you ask your secretary?"

"I sent her on a secret mission." He then explained the mission.

"Yes, I should have checked on that before I fired him. Go wait for your secretary, and let me know what she found out."

When Sandy got back she explained what to do with the papers, called Mary and reported that Mr. Perkins had been setting it up to do a little pilfering, but hadn't had time to do it yet. So on the first day things settled down to a routine for Smitty. Until Friday night.

Smitty didn't want to admit it but he was really nervous about meeting all of the family and friends of his bride-to-be. He strongly felt the class distinction. He confessed it to his secretary on Friday.

"That is just the bridegroom jitters. Everyone gets them. The good thing is that once you are married you can be mean to them or, even worse, ignore them because then they are just in-laws and nobody pays much attention to in-laws."

In the car on the way home, Mary said, "I got the finances straightened out. I'm glad you thought of it; it might have been a problem down the road. Are you excited about the party tonight?"

"I would rather be facing a blizzard in the mountains in my underwear than all those uppity people." Surprised at the outburst, Mary said with a smile, "I would never believe that you could be afraid of anything. What's so scary about a bunch of stuffed shirts?"

"I've been told not to get into any fights. To them I'm just an ex-marine country boy who has no right to be in your neighborhood. They know that if I hadn't saved your lives that Sonja would never think of marrying me. I think that myself most of the time." She looked at this giant of a man with the eyes of a mother who loves her little boy very much, "It's true that if it hadn't been for the plane crash we would probably not have met but now that we know you and have learned to love you we are not going to let you out of our lives even if we have to give up all of our friends to keep you. What would The Brick say if he were in your place?"

Smitty had to laugh at the thought. It was wonderful how Mary could always make him feel better. "He would say, 'If you don't like it, stand up so I can knock you down.' Or 'let's go outside and have a sporting event but it has to be four or more or it won't be a fair fight and I don't want to take advantage.'"

They kept up the banter the rest of the way home, making it hard for the eavesdropping chauffeur not to laugh out loud. The servants all liked the quiet easygoing Smitty. He seemed more like one of them, than one of the family.

CHAPTER FOURTEEN

S'mitty was as nervous as a long tailed cat in room full of mean dogs. Friday night had arrived and the welcome party had started. He felt about as welcome as a good case of the mumps. He stood where Mary told him to stand with Sonja beside him; as people came in, they were introduced to him. He felt like he was on display in some department store window and there was no way that he would ever remember all those names. If Sonja hadn't had a good grip on his arm he would have bolted. He was trying to look like he was enjoying himself but the things he could hear people say as they walked away were making him mad. Two old ladies said, "He is a big brute but not very handsome. I hear he hasn't any money either." Well, that was true enough. He was miserable. Then Sandy and her husband, Joe the truck driver, came in. They looked as uncomfortable as he felt, and that made him feel better.

They were finally called into dinner so he thought the pressure was off. Mary sat at the head of the table; she stood and said a little prayer of thanks for the food. When she had finished she looked around at everyone and said, "This party tonight has two purposes. The first as you know is to welcome Smitty to our circle of friends. The second is to announce the engagement of Sonja and Smitty." After each of these statements there was some polite clapping. "I don't plan to make a long speech here but I want everyone to know that I have grown to love Smitty just as if he were my own son. The fact that he rescued us from a slow and painful death only makes him more precious to me. Please welcome him as a member of the family. Now let's eat."

For some reason that little speech made him feel better; he didn't feel so much like an outsider. The party went pretty well after that. When they left the table he saw his secretary Sandy and her husband Joe and went over and thanked them for coming. Joe stated exactly what Smitty was experiencing, "I feel pretty out of place here with all of these stuffed shirts around me."

CHAPTER FIFTEEN

The night of the engagement party finally arrived. That same afternoon The Brick showed up with Shannon and Mr. Smith. Smitty was still at the office but Sonja was home and ran out to meet them when they drove up. "I am so glad to see you guys. I was worried that you might not make it. John, if you will wait here I will send somcone to get the bags and show you where to park the car. Okay?" John nodded and she led the others into the house. Soon the butler came out and helped The Brick unload the bags and pointed out a place to park the car. He explained that there would be a lot of people there tonight and parking would be tight. The Brick thought it looked like you could park a whole used car lot in that drive but said nothing as he and the butler carried the bags into the house.

When the limo arrived at the house Mary and Smitty went into the library to welcome the guests. Smitty said, "Hi everybody. Where is The Brick?" Shannon said, "He was mad because he couldn't wear his uniform to piss off the anti-war people, so he went out to tell his sad story to Sherpa. To save the peace, don't make fun of him." Smitty went out to see his two friends. He greeted his partner with a handshake and a slap on the shoulder then unhooked Sherpa from his chain and the three went for a walk around the grounds.

As they walked, Smitty told The Brick about the trouble at the office who asked him, "Do you think he waited for a blizzard to send the telegram, or did it just happen that way?"

"I don't know but I think Mary is checking into it."

"If it's true he should go to jail. If not, we should take care of it."

Smitty laughed. "I think we should wait and make sure of our facts first."

John changed the subject, "Boy, what a place, all those servants, a butler, a gardener, a couple of maids, a cook. Hey, can she cook?"

"Yes, she even took lessons. Mary made her."

"Did you hear? I wasn't allowed to bring my uniform to this shindig. Shannon rented me a suit. Just because of some hippy friends of Sonja's might be here."

"I think all of her friends are anti-war people. She didn't want any of her friends beating you up at our engagement party." John just snorted, "At least we would have some fun."

A lot of people showed up early. They too seemed to be expecting something, or maybe even planning it. During hors d'oeuvres one of Sonja's girlfriends came up to Smitty, "Well, Mr. Smith, how many women and children did you kill while you were over there?" Sonja came from across the room to his rescue. "I warned you that there would be no anti-war demonstrations at my house. Please leave." Before the girl could say anything, she raised her voice louder, "Now." The girl turned, said something to her boyfriend, and left. Another couple followed them out. Sonja raised her voice even more and said, "I warn everyone that I will not put up with any more rude nonsense at our party. If you have plans for some, please leave now. Things were quiet for a few minutes. People seemed to be a little shocked at her vehemence.

Then the conversational sounds resumed and the party

went on. Later Sonja told Smitty, "You see how much I love you; that girl that I ran off was my best friend, and maid of honor."

"I'm sorry honey. I wish I could help. I only have The Brick to stand with me. You could use Shannon. She will be here." So things were resolved. Everybody went home to wait for the wedding. John The Brick came in a suit that Shannon bought him. It looked good. She wore one of the blue bridesmaid dresses. Mary, wearing a pale green gown that went great with her auburn hair, looked so good that Smitty's dad couldn't keep his eyes off her.

The wedding went through without a hitch. She took him. He took her. There were no objections, etcetera. The wedding and reception were at the country club where her father had been a member. The reception went well. The Brick had too much to drink but so did a lot of people. The deed was done, and they were off on their honeymoon.

CHAPTER SIXTEEN

Mr. And Mrs. Smith returned from their honeymoon happy as clams at high tide. Mr. Smith went back to work at his fine job. Mrs. Smith called all her friends to chat about how great a time she had on her honeymoon; they chimed in with how beautiful she looked at the wedding. After completing the calls to everyone on her list of friends she jumped in her car and went to see her mother. There was a small holdup at the secretary's desk as Mary had some people in her office but Sonja was soon sitting in a nice chair in front of her mother's desk, telling Mary what a totally bad experience it had been calling her friends. While Sonja explained that her friends were upset with her for marrying a war veteran, Mary buzzed Smitty and told him to come to her office. After hugging his wife, he sat down and listened to his wife finish her story, half blaming him for all her sorrows.

"It's not Smitty's fault," Mary informed her daughter. "You knew who he was when you married him. You should get more grownup friends." Sonja started to say something but Mary waved her into silence and went on. "I'm glad you came in today. We have some family things to talk over that are more important than your feelings. When I returned from the mountains and took over the company, I started an investigation. I wanted to know who sent the urgent message that nearly got us all killed, and did kill my husband and the pilot. I just got the report from the agency. It looks like we're not through with Mr. Perkins yet. The message was: Very important that you return immediately. We have a serious problem: Perkins."

"So what was the big problem?" Smitty asked. "I haven't been able to find anything. I talked to Perkins secretary; she said she didn't even know that he had sent a message."

Sonja said, "Do you think he knew the blizzard was coming, and hoped that it would kill us?"

"I know that sounds crazy, but it's all I have been able to come up with."

"I don't suppose there is enough evidence to charge him with murder," Smitty said.

"No, the detective agency said we might try charging him with criminal negligence but wasn't sure we could prove it. That has taken all the fun out running this place. What are you thinking, Smitty? You look like you're going to explode."

"I'm thinking that I should send for The Brick and ask him to have a little chat with this wise guy. At least he would get the truth out of him." Both of the women smiled at the thought of The Brick's little chat and how much would be left of Perkins at the end of it. Mary said, "I like the idea, but I think we should stay on the legal side; however, I am ready to get out. We have had an offer to buy our shares at above market prices. We could sell our shares and the house without too much trouble and move to Lake Tahoe. What do you two think?"

Sonja said, "Well, I was thinking that I didn't want to move away from my friends but, after what happened this morning, I don't care anymore. Besides, I really like Shannon and she would be a good friend to me." Smitty said, "The Brick is getting out of the Marines and we need to get started on his house. We are also supposed to take over the mill soon. I was thinking that I would need to hire someone to take my place up there, but this would be a lot better and your gardener would probably be glad to get rid of Sherpa.”

“So, are The Brick and Shannon going to be staying at your place until their house is done?” Mary asked.

“No, she has an apartment in town. It will be closer for her to go to work from there.” And so the arrangements were made and they moved back to the mountains. The Brick and Shannon got married. The mill did well. Pretty much everything worked out for them all, especially for the gardener.

A few years later, as Shannon and The Brick were sitting in their porch swing admiring the beauty of the surrounding forest, Shannon mused, “It seems like a long time ago that Smitty rescued Mary and Sonja. I’m very happy that he did; they are my best friends.” He sighed, “Yeah, he rescued them but in a way they rescued him, too.”

“How’s that?”

“He was pretty down in the dumps after he lost his foot in Nam. They brought him back to life.” She looked at him and smiled “You are becoming quite the philosopher, John.” They both laughed. Life was good.

THE END

SALLY

CHAPTER ONE

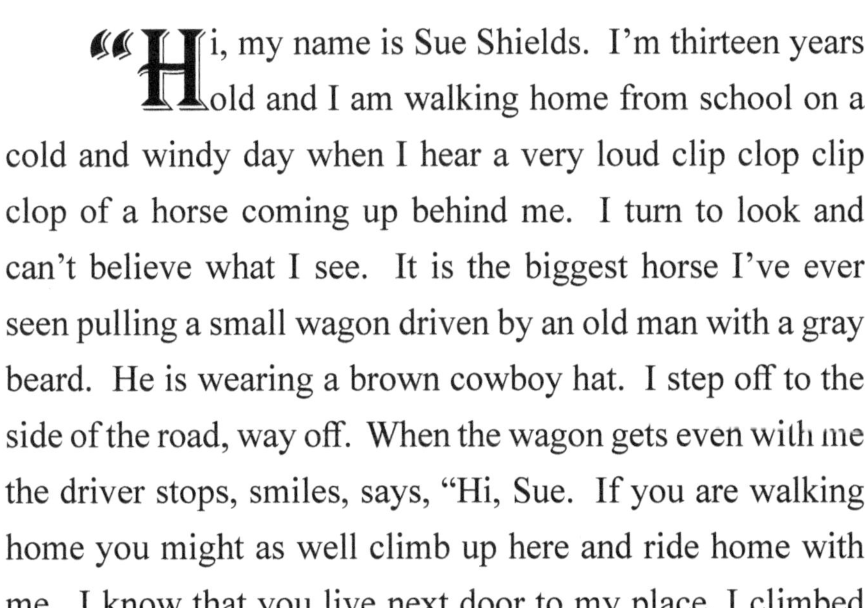

"Hi, my name is Sue Shields. I'm thirteen years old and I am walking home from school on a cold and windy day when I hear a very loud clip clop clip clop of a horse coming up behind me. I turn to look and can't believe what I see. It is the biggest horse I've ever seen pulling a small wagon driven by an old man with a gray beard. He is wearing a brown cowboy hat. I step off to the side of the road, way off. When the wagon gets even with me the driver stops, smiles, says, "Hi, Sue. If you are walking home you might as well climb up here and ride home with me. I know that you live next door to my place. I climbed up.

"That is the biggest horse I have ever seen. What's her name?"

"Her name is Sally. Say hi, Sally." Sally farted.

"That was rude, Sally." Sally tossed her head and snorted. I asked the old man, "Do you think she was laughing at us?"

"Yeah, I just got her and she has some bad habits. You don't look very warm. There is a jacket and a blanket in the box behind the seat." He reached back and opened the lid; I pulled them out. I was cold; I had on just a thin dress and sandals. Once I was all wrapped up in the coat and blanket and felt a lot better I said, "I saw you move in your camping trailer last spring and all of the work you did but I don't know your name."

"It's Jack. Jack Jones. And I'm glad to meet you, Sue. How come you had to walk home today? Miss the bus?"

"No, I am doing a report, and have to use the computer in the library so I have to walk home. If I had some warm clothes it wouldn't be so bad. It's only five miles."

"I don't mean to be forward, but I have a computer. If you wanted to use it you would only have to walk a hundred yards or so to get home."

"I don't know if my folks would like that, but I could

ask. What do you do for a living, other than building things on your place? Are you building a house now?"

"Well, to answer your first question, I am a retired carpenter. I get social security and retirement from the union. Now I write books and yes I am building a house."

"Do you need help? Winter is coming fast and I am a good worker. I need a job to buy some school clothes."

"I could use some help, but it's pretty hard work for a girl. I'm laying a block foundation and there is some heavy lifting."
Sally had started to pick up speed and was trotting fast. Jack pulled back on the reins, "Slow down, girl; we're not in that big of a hurry." She didn't like it but slowed to a sort of fast walk.

"I would like to try working for you and I would like to use your computer, too. How about after school tomorrow?"

"Yeah, sure. I'll leave the trailer open. I'll be working on my foundation but if you need anything just yell."
When we got to his place he drove the wagon to the barn and got down and opened the barn doors. He got back up on the wagon and spoke to Sally who backed the wagon into the barn with no trouble; he started to take off the harness. I said, "Wow, Sally acts like she knows just what she's doing. She backed it right in." I walked around to the front of her

and petted her long face and told her how pretty she was. Jack came up, took her bridle off and slipped on a halter that looked big enough for an elephant. I went back up on the wagon, folded the blanket, put it and the jacket back in the box and climbed down, said goodbye to Jack and Sally and headed for home. When I got there my dad yelled at me to get dinner going; he was hungry.

The next day at school I got together all the stuff I needed for my report and took it home on the bus. From the bus stop I ran down the road to Jack's place and went right to where he was working. "I brought all the stuff to work on my report; are you sure it's okay?"'

"Well, hello to you too, Sue. Yeah, I left the computer on so you shouldn't have any trouble."

"Thank you, Jack, and hi." Then I ran up to his camp trailer and went in. It was warm and felt real good, for I was still wearing that thin dress, and the wind was cold out there. His computer was set up where his dining table used to be. He had taken out the table and the right hand seat, and put in a computer desk with a big laptop with a separate key board and mouse. It was a good setup and I went right to work. An hour later I was about done but I didn't see any printer. I was about to go ask Jack what to do when I remembered how cold it was out. In the broom closet I found an old coat and put it on and went out to talk to Jack. Now Jack is over six feet tall and weighs about two hundred and fifty pounds so that coat could wrap around me twice at least but it was warm. When I got down to the new house site I told him, "Jack I finished my report, but I can't find your printer; what do I do?"

"It is about getting dark. When I finish cleaning up I'll come show you." I ran back to the trailer. The coat was warm but my legs were bare and the wind was still cold. Jack came in, opened the drawer in the desk and took out a flash drive. "Just put it on this and print it out at school." When I was done, I packed up my stuff and started to leave. He told me, "Wear the coat; you can bring it back tomorrow."

"What time do we start?"

"All right, you can work tomorrow. Be here at seven. If you're any kind of worker we could finish this weekend. See you in the morning."

I was up early, had some toast and was at the trailer at five to seven. I knocked; Jack yelled that it was open so I went in. IIc was at his desk eating a bowl of cereal. When he turned and looked at me, his eyes went to my bare legs; "You can't work dressed like that. Don't you have some long pants and boots?"

"No, all I own are three dresses and these sandals."

I did have on a ragged old sweat shirt. Now, I know that a dress and sandals don't sound too great for laying block, but it's all I had.

He sat staring at me for a while. "Okay, there are sheets in that closet. You can change the bed while I feed Sally. Put the dirty sheets in that dirty clothes bag on the bunk. We will go to town and wash clothes until the stores open then we will buy you some work clothes and boots. Don't worry. I'll take it out of your pay." I thought we were going to be riding the wagon to town but Jack pulled up in his blue truck. I lugged the clothes bag out and we headed for town. After the wash was done, folded, and stacked on the back seat of the truck, the thrift store was open.

"Pick out three or four pair of jeans, four or five work shirts, some boots and a belt and a jacket to work in." I was a little worried about spending that much money but did it anyway. He also got me some cowboy boots and tennis shoes for school. Then we went to a clothing store so the sales lady could fit me with a couple of bras and some tank tops and a couple of nice blouses.

I felt so pleased that I wanted to kiss that old man but he was so big and mean looking that I didn't dare. I got dressed in a bra, work clothes and boots at the store. With all of the rest of my plunder in bags in the back seat we headed for home. I told Jack that I felt bad about making him spend all that money, but he said, "If we work the rest of the weekend you will have earned enough to pay for it all and then some. That's the good thing about shopping at a thrift store."

When we got home we went right to work. Jack showed me how to mix mortar for laying block and then kept repeating, "I'm looking for some more mud," or "I'm looking for some more block." Those blocks are heavy. And did you know that a full bucket of mortar weighs eighty-five pounds? I took him a half a bucket at a time. By quitting time we had all the blocks laid. I even held the story pole while he shot in the top two corner blocks. By then I was so tired that I didn't even think I could walk home. He drove me and helped carry in all my stuff. My dad came into the front room to yell for his supper but when he saw how big Jack was he kept his mouth shut.

The next day I was at Jack's at six thirty and had ham and eggs with him. It took all day to pour the block full of concrete and put in the anchor bolts but it was ready now to start framing the house. Jack ordered pizza and by the time we got the mixer and tools cleaned up it was delivered. He sent me home with a big one for me and my dad so I wouldn't have to fix supper. I was too tired to do that, anyway. The next day was Monday and I looked good in my new jeans and blouse and cowboy boots and jacket. When I got to school I plugged in the flash drive and printed out my report. It looked almost as good as me.

That next week every night after school I would check to see how much Jack had got done. It was hard to believe how much work that old man could do. He fell a bunch of trees up on the hill, cut them into logs the lengths that he needed, took Sally up there, pulled the logs down to his little band sawmill and started cutting them into the lumber to build his house. When Saturday came I helped him pour the slab in his basement. That took all day. Actually, I helped pour the slab. That only took a couple of hours. The rest of the day was spent finishing it. Jack did that. That evening Jack paid me what he owed me after he took out for the clothes; I still had a bunch of money left. I was excited.

"I'm going to church tomorrow; would you like to come?"

"What do I wear?"

"What you wear to school is fine. Wear your jacket, though. I'm going on my scooter and it is getting a bit late in the season for that." We rode the scooter. It is real cute. It is candy apple red and goes pretty fast. After church we went for lunch at the local café in town. One of the high school boys that I had seen at church was there with his family. He kept looking over at us.

When we were done eating, while Jack was paying the bill, I went outside and put on Jack's motorcycle helmet. It was too big but it was required for anyone under eighteen. The high school boy came out and walked over and introduced himself. "Hi, I'm Bob Short. I saw you at church. Do you go often?"

"No, that was the first time for me. Jack goes a lot."

"What's your name?"

"Sue Shields."

"Is Jack your dad?"

"No, he is my neighbor. He is building a house and I am helping him."

"That must be nice having a real pretty girl to help. Do you think he could use some more help?"

"Ask him yourself. Here he comes."

"Good afternoon, sir. I'm Bob Short. Sue says you're building a house. Could you use some help? I'm a pretty good carpenter."

"Yes, I do need help but are you sixteen yet?"

"I will be next month."

"Well, here is my card. Come see me next month."

"Jack fired up that pretty scooter and we took off. When we got to my house Jack let me off and I gave him back his helmet. I asked, "What was that about being sixteen?"

"It's the law. You have to be sixteen to work in construction. I think he just wanted to be here near you. He probably won't be any good as a worker just standing around staring at you." Before I could hit him with anything he revved up his motor and took off for home.

When the next Saturday came around, I was at Jack's trailer at six thirty, just in time for breakfast. Ham and eggs again. With some hot tea and toast with jam, it was plenty good. We went to the barn. He handed me a pair of leather gloves; as he harnessed Sally, he told me, "If you're going to work you need gloves to keep your hands from getting torn up."

"Thank you. What are we doing today anyway?"

"Dragging logs to the mill. Hand me that single tree,will you?"

"Sure. What's a single tree?" A voice behind me said, "I'll get it" and Bob Short walked past me and picked up a long round pole with two hooks on one side and a ring on the other. He handed it to Jack and helped hook it to Sally's harness. Jack had a big shit eating grin on his face as he hooked a big logging chain to the ring on the single tree. I knew that grin was going to make me mad so I decided to take it out on Bob. I asked him in an angry voice,

"What are you doing here?"

"One, I wanted to see what the job was. Two, this isn't your house. And three, I wanted to see if you were as cute as I remembered."

Before I could say anything Jack pushed the reins into my hands and picked up the chain, "Get up, Sally" and we were off to the woods to haul logs. I was almost pulled off my feet with Sally's first step but I pulled on the left rein and ran to keep up all the way up to the woods.

When we got to the logs that he had ready he turned Sally around. While pulling on the chain he said, "Back Sally, back." When she had gone far enough he stopped her and hooked up the chain to the log. Then he told Bob and me, "I wrote a number on each log. I need them brought down by those numbers, because I need to cut the lumber that I need last, first. Do you two think you can do that all by yourselves? Watch out for the logs rolling. Stay up beside the horse." He handed the reins to Bob and picked me up and threw me up on Sally's back and, with a big grin on his face, walked off down the hill. Bob said, "Get up," and Sally leaned into the harness and we headed down to the saw mill. We made trip after trip with me on the reins and Bob on the chain on the uphill run and Bob on the reins and me riding on the downhill run. Sally's back is so wide and flat that you have to hang on to the harness to stay on. Jack was running the band saw mill, cutting lumber and stacking it. When he had a stack ready he would pick it up with the forks on the front of his backhoe and put it in the barn to dry.

At lunch time we stopped to eat. I asked Jack, "Why is it alright for us to haul logs but not to do construction?"

"Moving logs with a horse is considered farm work, and its okay for little brats to do farm work."

"Little brats? Why, you whisker puss old coot, if I wasn't having so much fun I'd quit."

"If you did that, you wouldn't be able to flirt with Bob and get paid for it, too. Poor guy." With that he scooted out the door before I could throw anything at him.

When we got back to Sally we gave her water and headed back up the hill. We worked until dark. When we got back to the barn we took the harness off and hung it up in the barn. We climbed up to the loft and pitched hay down to the manger. Bob asked Jack, "How much does she get?"

"About twice as much as a regular horse. I will get her a bucket of grain to go with her hay."

We could hear Jack down in the stall with Sally, brushing her. He yelled up at us, "If you guys are up there more than five minutes, I'll come up and separate you." I grabbed up the pitchfork and headed for the stairs, but Bob stopped me and took it away and threw it in the hay pile. Now he was the one with the shit eating grin. As we went down the stairs, I was still looking for something to hit Jack with. When we got to Sally's stall Jack said, "Well, tomorrow is Sunday. I guess we will see you at church, huh Bob?" I said something about him being a mean old man but Jack just kept brushing. Bob said, "Well, I'll be there and it would be nice to see you there too, Sue." I headed for home.

Sunday morning found me at Jack's trailer at eight. That's when he leaves to eat breakfast at the VFW. I had on my best jeans on and my best blouse. I had fixed my hair real nice and shined my cowboy boots. It was the best I could do. That damned old Jack is right about me liking Bob and it seems like I'm going to have to put up with Jack so I can see Bob.

Jack doesn't talk much; you have to ask questions to get any information so at breakfast I asked, "Are you married, Jack?"

"Widower with two kids and five grandkids. They all live over by Seattle. Any more questions, nosey?"

"Yes, why don't you live over there near them?"

"I don't like the rain and I was born here and wanted to retire here. Is that okay with you?"

"Yeah. You know, I don't like you much. You tease

too much, but I like Sally." One of Jack's friends came by our table to say hi and asked, "Who's your girlfriend?"

"Just some skinny kid that came by my place. I thought I had better feed her."

I informed the friend, "I'm his neighbor. I'm Sue and he can be a jerk sometimes."

"You got that right, Sue. What do you want to be seen with him for?"

"He's buying breakfast."
We stayed around until almost ten. His friends were just as bad as Jack at teasing me. I didn't know that old guys were all like that. Obviously I need younger friends.

We went to church. It was time for Sunday school and I lied and said I was in high school so I could be in Bob's class. He didn't know how old I was; I was built good enough to get away with it. He sat with me. I was so excited that I didn't listen much to what was being said. In church I sat with Jack and Bob came and sat next to me. Jack had his stupid grin again but I decided to ignore him. I liked the singing. I sing pretty well and so did Bob. Jack didn't. After church Bob introduced me to his family; they already knew Jack. We all went to lunch together.

At lunch, Bob told his folks about Sally and hauling logs and about lifting me up on her back to ride back. Bob's father asked Jack, "Do you pay these two for playing with your horse all day?"

"Yes, but the horse needs the exercise and I need the logs."

On the way home, I forgave Jack for all the teasing. I had never had two better days in my whole life and I think Bob was beginning to like me, too. That next Monday while I was waiting for the bus after school, I saw Jack drive by in his truck so I walked to the grocery store. When I found him I said that I needed to buy some more clothes and asked if I could ride home with him. He was waiting at the truck when I came out of the store. I put my packages in the back seat with his groceries. Driving home he asked, "What did you get?"

"Two skirts, two more blouses, some stockings, and a nice jacket for church. I noticed that everyone dresses nice for church except you so I thought I needed some better clothes."

"Do you think Bob will notice and like you better?"

"I hope so, but it's not just for him. It's to make me feel better about myself."

"I can understand that but you don't need to worry about it. You are a very pretty girl and even though they say that clothes make the girl, a nice figure makes all the difference in the world."

"Do you think I'm pretty, Jack?"

"Yeah, and your long hair is pretty, too. With long hair and a nice figure you don't even have to be pretty to catch a guy so you got it all."

"Thanks, Jack, that's very nice of you to say so."

"It's the truth and I always tell the truth except when I don't."

When we reached home, Jack went to work at the mill and worked until dark. It rained a couple of days that week so Jack worked on his book writing. The rest of the week he cut lumber and moved it into the barn. When Saturday came I was at Jack's trailer in time for breakfast and Bob showed up about seven and we went to the barn to harness Sally. She wasn't done eating her breakfast so while we waited for her we sat on a hay bale and talked. Bob put his arm around me and asked if he could kiss me. I said, "Please do," and he did. We hauled logs until about four, finishing everything that was cut. We put Sally back in her stall after taking off her harness and hanging it up. We then went up to the loft and pitched hay down for her and got her some grain, too, stopping to kiss once in a while. I loved it.

Jack worked late at the mill. Bob and I stickered and stacked the lumber and Bob moved it into the barn with the backhoe.

The next Sunday I got dressed in my new clothes and was at Jack's trailer at eight in time to go to the VFW for breakfast. After we finished eating and were sitting around drinking coffee with his friends, Jack handed me a wrapped package. I opened it. It was a Bible in a red cover with my name in gold letters printed on it. All I could say was thank you. We went to church; when they said to open your Bible, I did. I even listened in Sunday school even though Bob sat next to me. He sat next to me in church, too, and after church in the restaurant, too. We ate with his family again. When we went outside to wait for the rest of them Bob asked if he could tell everyone that I was his girl. I said yes. When Jack came out I think I was wearing his stupid grin. I hope it looked better on me than it did on him.

The next few weeks went by. When all the logs were made into lumber Jack started the house. It was also November and it started to snow. The next Sunday on the way to breakfast Jack said, "I think I will wait a few weeks and let the lumber dry out some more before I start framing the house. My publisher is after me to finish this book I'm working on."

"What's it about?"

"About Vietnam and some of the good stuff that we

did there."

"What do you mean, good stuff? I thought all you did was kill people."

"We built houses for refugees, good roads, water systems, and hospitals. They didn't even have a road from north to south to tie the country together until we built it. We lost that war because of the media and our government's fear of Russia and China. If we fought the Second World War like they made us fight that one we would all be speaking German or Japanese."

"Don't get mad. I'm sorry I said anything. Look, I brought my Bible." He didn't answer; he just growled. I think it was good that he was writing about the war. It might get it out of his system, and make him more human. He was quiet at breakfast. At least I didn't get teased.

Church went well with Bob sitting beside me. At lunch Jack started talking again. "If this snow keeps up, I'm going to have to clear some driveways." Bob's dad, whose name is John, asked, "What do you have to do it with, a snow blower?"

Bob responded, "No, he has a backhoe and it is four wheel drive. Hey, can you put runners on your wagon and do sleigh rides?"

"No, but once the roads are clear I can give wagon

rides."

"I take it that you have the time." John asked, "What do you do for a living?"

"I'm retired and I write books."

"What are you writing about now?" I jumped in with, "Don't ask. He'll get all fired up again."

"Don't listen to her. I'm writing about Vietnam. Earlier she said all we did was kill people over there. That would make any vet angry."

"My dad was there and talked about trying to help the people," John said. "It was a bad deal."

On the way home I asked Jack, "In Sunday school they talked about the Philippian jailer. He said "What must I do to be saved?" and they said, "Believe on the Lord Jesus Christ and though shall be saved." Is that all there is to it?"

"Yeah, that's pretty much it."

"Come on. Give me the rest of it. There has to be more."

"They want you to say a little prayer so repeat after me: Dear Jesus, I would like you to come into my life and forgive me of my sins so I can be with you in heaven. Thank you, amen." I repeated it after him and then asked, "Am I a Christian now?"

"Yes. How do you feel?"

"I feel fine. How do you feel?"

"I feel fine, too. It's nice to have you in the family." When we got home I couldn't wait to call Bob and tell him what happened. I did it on Jack's phone because my dad wouldn't have liked it. Jack went out and started the tractor while we talked. Bob was happy for me; he said that now he didn't have to pray that I would be saved any more. And he said that he loved me. After we hung up Jack gave me a ride home on the backhoe and cleared our driveway.

It kept snowing. That week every night after school I stopped at Jack's house and we studied the Bible for a while. Come to find out he was a missionary and knows his Bible. When we got to the VFW on Sunday, Bob met us there for breakfast. Jack said it was just because he was paying for it but I knew it was because Bob and I were in love. I asked Bob, "Did you know that Jack was a missionary?" at which Jack corrected me, "I was just a missionary builder, building in Africa and France. I wasn't a preacher."

"Well, that's a lot." Bob said.

In Sunday school I told everyone about becoming a Christian on the way home the week before and about studying the Bible with my ex-missionary neighbor. We talked about it the whole time. Everyone congratulated me. Bob sat with me looking very happy both in Sunday school and in church, too. I have never been happier in my life.

It snowed on and off for the next two weeks. We studied the Bible after school and Jack worked on his book and cleared driveways. Jack set up his planer and router tables in the barn and started working on the boards for the floor. He had to plane them down to the same thickness and, on his router table, tongue and groove them which was a lot of work.

One night after Bible study, Jack said, "If it isn't snowing tomorrow, I will start framing the house. Saturday you and Bob can help."

"If it's not snowing. Good. I am looking forward to working on your house. I can't wait to see it finished. Are you going to build a garage?"

"Yes, but separate from the house and not till next year."

When Saturday came I was at the trailer at six thirty for ham and eggs again. Bob came at seven. By then Jack had moved some lumber from the barn down to the house. He already had the basement framed up and was ready for the floor joists. By the end of the day we had the sub floor down and I was tired. That's hard work.

On Sunday we met at the VFW again for breakfast. I asked Jack, "Won't the snow bother the wood?"

"Not if you sweep it off before it melts. It's cold enough outside so it will be fine,"
At lunch after church Bob's dad was teasing us by checking on our usefulness. "How are the kids working out for you on your house building?"

"They are doing fine. I think Sue is a better carpenter than Bob but together they did well." Bob just grinned. He takes Jack's teasing better than I do.
I reminded Jack that all I did was haul lumber. "I didn't lift a hammer."

By the end of the month the outside of the house was done. Jack said he didn't like plumbing so he hired a plumber to do it while he did the electrical. In another month with Bob and me helping with the dry wall and the painting and the finish work the house was done. Jack had some furniture in storage so we helped him move in. I proposed, "We should have a house warming party and invite the whole church." Bob agreed but Jack said, "You two should buy all the refreshments. You got rich hanging around here watching me work." We laughed. I was getting used to his jokes. At the VFW the next Sunday we told his old friends about the party and we told the pastor to announce it at church so we spent the next Saturday getting ready.

The party went well. Bob and I did all the work and

Jack paid for it. He bought a pool table for the basement and put his computer desk down there near the wood stove. I would go over on Saturday and clean his house for him and do his laundry, too. He always paid me. When spring came we built a two car garage with Bob's help. Jack and Sally plowed and planted five acres of alfalfa then Bob and I fenced it in to keep Sally out of it. We also plowed and disked a large garden area then planted it. All summer we had to keep the weeds out and water in but it did really well.

Four years went by with pretty much the same routine. Then one summer day Jack took his backhoe down to the creek to make a pond. The creek was on his property so he didn't ask anybody if it was all right. He just started digging. He hadn't got very far when he dug up some bones. At first he thought about not telling anyone but then he decided he better call the cops. After calling 911 and telling them his story he walked up to his house to wait for a sheriff deputy to come. When one came he introduced himself as Don Grover. "So, you were digging a pond and dug up some bones. How long have you lived here?"

"About five years, but there is no meat on the bones so I figure they been here a while."

"Who owned the place before you?"

"I don't remember their names, but it's in the paperwork

from when I bought it. It's at the house." They walked up to the house to look at the papers and wait for the detective to show up. It took a while. Jack made coffee and they drank a few cups while they waited. When Detective Bill Ellis got there they went down to the hole in the ground that Jack had started and looked at the bones. What he had dug up was an arm and hand. In the side of the hole you could see part of a rib cage showing. Detective Ellis said to wait for the forensic team to show up. So they went up to the house and drank more coffee.

It's a good thing he had started early. When they got there they looked at the bones and asked Jack if he could dig down close to the body with the backhoe so that they didn't have to dig it all by hand. He did. When they had the whole body uncovered they could see by the dress it was wearing that it was a woman. Or a cross dresser. No, the forensic people said it was female. They packed up the bones and told Jack not to do anymore digging until they told him he could. They wanted to dig around for evidence. They all left and Jack went to the barn to feed Sally. After that he went to the house to make dinner. He put on a big pot of chili and was waiting for it to cook when Bob and I showed up. I asked, "What were the cops doing here?" Jack told us the story and showed us the picture he took on his phone. I suddenly felt sick. Bob said, "What's the matter, honey?"

"That kind of looks like a dress of my mother's. She just disappeared about ten years ago. I kind of wondered why we never heard from her. I always thought she didn't like me."

"Now, you don't know for sure that is her. We better wait for the cops to check into it." Jack said.

"What if it is her? Does that make my dad the killer? I don't want to go home. What if he saw the cops over here? Will he run?"

Bob said, "Calm down, honey. We don't know anything for sure. I'll take you to town to get some clothes so you can stay here if that's okay with you, Jack. Do you need money?"

"No, I keep my money here so my dad can't get it. He would go on a big drunk and that would be the end of my money. Can I stay here, Jack?"

"Yeah sure, but don't say anything to anyone about this; it could get back to your dad. Will he miss you if you are not home tonight?"

"No, I left him a sandwich. I planned to stay out late with Bob anyway.
We went to town in Bob's truck. On the way he comforted me with, "I really hope it's not your mom. I have some

good news, though. I got a job at the saw mill today. I start on Monday. I will be making enough money so we can get married, if you will have me."

"Oh yes! Where will we live?"

"I rented a one bedroom cabin that the mill owns. It's small but there is just the two of us. I am excited. How about you?"

"I would have to ask my dad since I'm a minor."

"You can get married in Washington when you are sixteen. We can go there. It's only forty miles; our friends would drive that far. What do you say?"

"Let's do it."

At the thrift store I bought some clothes to keep at Jack's house and, while Bob was looking at furniture, I tried on a wedding dress. It fit perfectly. I paid for it all and told them to hold the wedding dress for Jack to pick up. I didn't want Bob to see it. I didn't know it at the time but the next day Jack went to town to see about being a foster parent for me just in case my dad had to go away. Jack had plenty of money and he knew all of the county big shots on a first name basis so it should work out or so I hoped.

It was a week later when the cops finally got around to questioning me. Detective Ellis came to Jack's house and we sat down in the living room. He showed me the pictures of the bones and asked, "Do you think you might know who this is?"

"My mother had a dress like that. She left us about ten years ago. Do you think it might be her?"

"We don't know who it is yet. Have you ever heard from her at all?"

"No, and I always wondered why. Mom and dad fought a lot but they both drank too much. I always thought she left because she was mad at me and that was why I never heard from her. I missed her a lot."

"Did she ever have any broken bones that you remember?"

"Yes, she broke her arm once; I don't remember how. I think it was her left arm, but I'm not sure. Come to think of it, she didn't take any of her clothes with her. When I asked why, dad said she didn't like them."

"Do you think that your dad did it?"

"I hope not; he's all I have left. Do you have any leads? I know it's been ten years. I hope it's not my mom. I hope she's on a beach somewhere in Hawaii."

The detective thanked everyone and left. I turned to Jack and told him my news, "Bob asked me to marry him. He got a job at the saw mill and rented a cabin.

"Are you going to ask your dad for permission?"

"I don't think so. Bob says you can get married in Washington when you're sixteen and I'm seventeen. What did you do with my wedding dress?"

"It's in my closet. I don't think anyone will look in there."

So we went to Washington, got a license and set it up for the next Saturday. Bob went to work at the mill on Monday and Jack and I went furniture shopping. He paid for most of it. What the thrift store didn't have we got at other places: dishes, pots and pans and sheets and blankets. Bob's folks donated a lot, too. It took us most of the week. Then we went food shopping and stocked the cupboards and refrigerator with everything we could think of. I made sure dad had plenty of booze so he would be too drunk to notice. I stayed at Jack's house and took food over to dad every day. On Saturday, Bob's sister, Ellen, came over and helped me get ready. She curled my hair and helped with the dress and Jack drove me to the church and walked me down the aisle. It was so exciting that I had a hard time saying I do but I got it said and the preacher said, "You may kiss the bride, and I would like to introduce Mr. and Mrs. Bob Short."

It was the most wonderful time in my life. The reception was at the VFW hall. Jack's friends complained that the bar was closed but they all wanted to kiss the bride and dance with her. Even the Sheriff's Department was there. At least, I saw Deputy Grover and Detective Ellis there. The food was catered and good; the cake was enormous. Then we drove to the cabin in Bob's truck. I'll leave the rest of the night to your imagination. We made it to church the next day.

The routine of our lives started with me driving Bob to the mill and then driving to Jack's house to clean and cook for dad and Jack. I was even using Jack's washer and dryer for dad's laundry and mine, too. This only lasted a week. Detective Ellis showed up one day. I invited him in for coffee. We all sat down in the front room and after I had served the coffee he said, "I have some bad news. The forensic people say the bones are your mother's. We are going to arrest your father. We are convinced that he killed her. I am real sorry that I'm the one to have to tell you. On the other hand, I'm glad that you are married and not living at home anymore."

I told the detective, "I thought all along that that might be the case but I was still hoping that I was wrong. Thank you for coming to tell me. Now if you will excuse me I think I need to go cry a little. Where will you take him?"
"To Priest River for now. After the trial, if he is convicted, he will go to Boise. Again, I'm sorry to bring you the bad news." I went up to my old room and sat on the bed and

cried. When I heard the detective leave, Jack came up and sat on the bed beside me and put his arm around me. He didn't say anything. He just held me for a while. After a while he said, "It's about time for you to pick up Bob. Don't come tomorrow. Tell Bob to drive himself to work. I will pick you up about ten if you like. I have something to show you."

He was there at ten. When I got into his truck he asked me, "What did Bob say when you told him?"

"That he was sorry. Did you know that he has never met my dad? Did you take some food over to him last night?"

"No, after you went upstairs he told me that they had already taken your father so I'm sure they fed him. All that I can say is that I'm sorry."

"I'm mostly upset that dad killed my mom. I know it hasn't been proven but I remember how guilty he acted and that she didn't take anything with her when she left. It even looked funny to a seven year old." We drove to the house of a friend of Jack's and got out. His friend came out.

"About time you came to pick that thing up. I was about to have it towed away."

We went over to a nice blue Subaru. Jack smiled broadly and announced, "I bought this for you. I had it registered in your name and mine. It's insured under my policy so you won't have to worry about it. Here are the keys. Get in and take it home."

I was still feeling kind of out of it. "Is this for me?"

"Yeah, your name is on the title so if you don't like it take it and trade it for a Ford." So I got in and took off. It hadn't soaked in yet but it did on the way home. I called him on his cell phone and asked, "Why?"

"You are more like my family than my family and you needed a car."

"Thank you, Jack. From now on you're my family. And I love you."

"I love you, too." And he hung up.

Four months later, while I was cleaning Jack's house one day, he asked me, "Are you gaining weight?"

"Isn't that what's supposed to happen when you're pregnant?"

Jack said that he was driving into Sand Point the next day. Since I only cleaned his house once a week, I asked to go along. It's the biggest town around here and the best shopping so I wanted to go, too. He bought every piece of baby furniture he could find. I told him that I didn't have room in my house for all of that and made him put some of it back. He bought a play-pen and a walker for his house, for when we were there and for when I wanted him to baby-sit.

I went to see my dad a couple of times before the trial. It was the first time I had seen him sober in years. I asked if there was anything he needed and he said no. I told the detective that I wouldn't testify against him. He said I didn't have to because when they arrested him and searched the house they found a box in the garage that was full of her stuff: her purse with her driver's license, her jewelry box, shoes, clothes and everything she would want with her when she left.

The trial didn't go well for him. Jack and I went to watch. He got twent-five years to life. It was the last time I was to see him. I don't remember ever loving him; he was drunk all the time and living on disability. The house was a rental so the people who owned it asked if I wanted anything out of it. I said no.

When the baby was born we named him Jack Edward Short. We had two more boys and a girl. When the second baby was born Jack moved into the basement with his pool table and wood stove and we took over the rest of the house. When Jack got too crippled up with arthritis to work his gardens anymore, he sold Sally, the wagon and the farm implements. When he was eighty he died of a heart attack. In his will he left the farm to us. To each of his kids he left some money and some for me, too. I would get a yearly check for the rest of my life. We had known Jack for fifteen years. In all those years we had never wanted for anything that he didn't immediately provide for us. He spoiled us and we loved him. Good bye, Jack. We'll miss you.

THE END

SPY STORY

CHAPTER ONE

It was pouring rain in Los Angeles. When I got to the airport, I got soaked just getting from the taxi to the terminal. As I checked my bag I heard a man standing near me say that the Los Angeles River actually had some water running in it. I got my ticket and my temporary FBI identification got me through security. Having a first class ticket got me on the plane first so I was seated with my briefcase on my lap going through some papers when a very beautiful girl took the seat beside me. She had long black wavy hair, dark brown eyes and a very nice figure, maybe a little top heavy, if that's possible. Her clothes were expensive looking though I'm no expert. She looked like she might be Arabian; the paper that I was reading was in Arabic. She glanced over at it, looked at me and greeted me in Arabic. I returned the greeting. She asked where I was from. I told her that I lived in New York but that I was from Jerusalem originally. She was asking too many questions.

I am a Massad Agent undercover with the FBI. Massad is the Israeli secret service and has the best trained agents in the world, according to the KGB anyway. I introduced myself, using my undercover name, "I am Bob Carson on my way home from a business conference in LA. I'm glad that a beautiful woman is sitting next to me instead of a fat old business man."

"I am Carman Abdula on a trip around America. I am glad that I'm not sitting next to a fat old business man, too."

"You are traveling without a chaperone?"

"She is back in coach. My father doesn't want to pay for first class for her."

The stewardess came by to ask if we wanted anything to drink. I would have liked to have some wine but Arabs don't drink, so I ordered a coke. So did she.

I asked her, "Where have you been so far?"

"We went across the country on the train, stopping here and there to see the sights. I think next I would like to see the New England states and eat lobster in Maine."

"What did you like best?"

"The northwest, especially the mountains and the lakes. They are so lovely. We don't have anything as pretty as that in Israel."

The plane was getting ready to take off; the stewardess told us to fasten our seatbelts and gave us lunch menus. The food on these flights was pretty good. We both ordered steak. And tea. No wine. After we had eaten she told me about her father who was one of the leaders of a Palestinian groups in Israel. This was interesting. I was here in America working with the FBI getting information on those groups working in America.

"Is your father going to meet you when we land?"

"I don't think he knows what our schedule is so I don't think so. Do you have anyone meeting you, like a wife?"

"I am not married. I travel so much on business that it would be tough. Why do you ask? Are you applying for the job?"

"Well, let's see: you're nice looking. You must be Palestinian even though you don't look it; you have no beard, but you speak the language. Do you come from a good family?"

"No. I am an orphan. Does that ruin it for me?"

"Yes. Sorry. If you aren't from a good family there's no hope unless you have a lot of money. Then maybe you could talk my father into it but it would have to be a lot of money."

We both laughed. We talked all the way across the country. By the time we landed we were great friends and, if it were not an impossible situation, I would say that I was in love. It isn't often you meet a girl who is not only beautiful but funny and sexy and charming, too. Sometimes life isn't fair.

While the plane taxied to the terminal we got her carry-on bag; I carried her bag and my briefcase as we walked off the plane together. I searched the other passengers for the chaperone and thought I found her. She was an older woman, dressed nicely but with mean eyes. You might say chaperone eyes. As the luggage came down the ramp Carman showed me which bags to get. Getting the luggage cart proved to be a good idea: I had only one bag, the chaperone had two. Carman had eight. As I was loading the bags two men with rags wrapped around their heads came over and started talking to Carman and the chaperone. By the time I got all the bags on the cart they were arguing in Arabic. I walked over and, using a phony southern drawl, asked "What's the problem, ma-am?"

She looked worried. "These men say that my father sent them but I don't know them and I don't believe them." I was standing behind them so I cracked their heads together and let them slump to the floor. I decided not to kill them in case they actually were from her father. We then headed for the door, with me pushing the cart. I didn't want to hang around and explain things to the cops. Out on the sidewalk I saw a limo driver that I knew and headed for his car. Two more rag heads tried to grab Carman, but the limo driver conked one with a sap and I chopped the other one in the neck. A cop standing a little way off came over; while the driver got the women and the bags into the car, I showed him my FBI identification and we drove off.

Carman got on her cell phone, placed a call, and started talking fast in Arabic. When she hung up I commented, "You look upset. Is there something I can do?"

"Yes, do you know a safe place we can stay? My father says it is not safe to come to his hotel. Some enemies of his are all over his hotel. He thinks they are trying to take me to force him to do something he doesn't want to do." I looked at the driver, "Is there someplace they would be safe?" He rolled up the window between us and started talking on his cell phone. In just a few minutes he turned the car onto a freeway, rolled the window down, and assured us that he would take us to a safe place. "If you will tell me your father's name and what hotel he is in I will see what we can do about those enemies of his." She quickly responded, "His name is Mobu Abdula and he is at the Palace." He rolled the window up again and talked on his phone for about five minutes while we drove out to the suburbs. While we drove she told me that her father was the leader of a Palestinian group that is not trying to blow up America, and that some of the other groups were trying to get him to help them with some project that seems important to them, which was just the kind of thing the FBI had hired me to work on.

We ended up in a nice neighborhood in front of a large house with a high wall around it and a locked gate. The driver punched in a code on a stand and the gate opened; we drove through to the house. The driver went to the front door and took out a big ring of keys, found the right one, and opened the door. He came back and opened the door for the ladies. "The rooms are at the top of the stairs. Pick out the one you want and I will bring up your bags." Carman asked for directions to a restroom, to which he responded, "Each room has its own bath."

He and I started hauling bags into the house and upstairs to the rooms. While outside I checked with him, "Am I staying here, too?"

"Yes, they might need protection. If you will have the women make out a shopping list I will go to the store and get food and whatever else they might need so they won't have to go out until we clear out some of Papa's enemies. Oh, there's a pool out back so if they don't have bathing suits have them put that on the list too." I went to tell them to make a list of the things we would need, knowing that Arab women didn't go swimming, at least not where a man could see them, but just out of orneriness I told them what the driver said about swim suits. They both stared at me but then Carman smiled and said in English, "I am tempted. I have always been jealous of Christian women being able to run around in swim suits in front of men."

"When in Rome do as the Romans do or just wait until after dark and go skinny dipping."

"I don't know what that means, but I can guess. I do have shorts and a top that would work but only if you promise not to look." I started looking around the front room like I was searching for something.

"Do you promise? What are you looking for?"

"Oh yeah, I promise. I'm looking for a good place to set up my movie camera."

"You are not funny."

"That's too bad. I was hoping to get a job as a comedian.

Do you know how to cook or does your friend? I am not a very good cook. We are going to have to eat here for now."

"Yes, my friend is a good cook. I will make sure that everything she needs is on the list. Is there anything you want for yourself?"

"Yes, root beer and cheese crackers, 7 Up and Coca Cola."

She made out a long list; when I took it to the driver he instructed me to take their cell phones away from them and turn mine off. "They could use GPS to find us and we don't know how determined they are to get her." I went in and found the women exploring the house; I relayed his instructions, "We need to turn off our cell phones. Your father's friends could use the GPS to locate us. If we need to use a phone, we will use the land line."

"Do you think that we are in danger? And how do we know whose side you are on or, as far as that goes, who your driver is?"

I just stared at her for a few seconds. "If you don't trust me, call your father or we can take you to his hotel if you like. Those men at the airport were not after me."
Her chaperone started talking real fast. "Apologize to him quickly. He has saved us twice already and we have to trust someone."

Carman smiled, "I apologize. Mahoni is right. We don't have a lot of options. We are both afraid and you and I have just met. There is no reason why you should put yourself in danger on our account."

"It's my job, but even if it wasn't I would want to stay here just to be with you. Do you know why they are after you?"

"Mahoni thinks it's because I travel around without a male relative as an escort. I'm a Muslim but some of the rules are a bit too much. You are from Palestine so you know the rules."

"Yes. I think Mohammed hated women." I said this in English which Mahoni didn't understand too well. When the driver got back, two other agents came in another car. They carried in the groceries and Mahoni started dinner. The driver, whose name was John Peterson, and I went outside and made a tour of the grounds. I noticed that there were some video cameras around. I asked him where the monitors were; "They're in a room in the basement. One of the other agents is there now so smile. You're on candid camera."

I went to the basement to see how much of the grounds were covered by the cameras. After ascertaining how everything worked I went upstairs to check on the wonderful smells coming from the kitchen. Mahoni demanded that I get out of the kitchen. I warned her that if she was mean to me, I would take over the cooking and everyone would suffer. Although very hard to believe, she actually smiled. Dinner was served in the dining room for all but the two agents who stayed on watch. They would eat later when they were relieved.

CHAPTER TWO: DOMESTIC BLISS

After a few days we had a regular routine going with watches set and all surveillance covered. Carman and I spent a lot of time talking together. I just liked looking at her; talking with her gave me an excuse. Sometimes she stayed with me in the room with the monitors when it was my turn on watch. Our meals were all taken together; the food was so good that I had to keep exercising to keep from gaining weight. When I was jogging around the property she sometimes went with me.

I thought that she was becoming fond of me. She asked me every now and then if I thought I had enough money to impress her father. One night while on watch in the monitor room I left to go to the bath room. When I came back she stood up as if she was going out but as she started to walk by me she turned at the last minute, put her arms around my neck and kissed me. It was not just a little peck; it was a we-are-getting-married-in-June type of kiss. When we finally unwrapped from each other I whispered, "I am very much in love with you. Do you feel the same?"

"Yes, the question is do you have enough money to make it okay with my father?"

"I don't know but there are worse complications than that. I can't go back to Israel." We sat down and I told her my long sad story which goes like this: "I got fed up with all the rules of the Muslim religion after they killed my sister for kissing her boyfriend in public. I became a Christian and then an American citizen. I now work full time for the FBI so you see how impossible our love is. Do you think your father could forgive me for all that even if I did have a lot of money?"

"No. If we got married the Palestinians would probably try to kill us both." We kissed some more anyway. She spent every watch with me from then on. About two weeks later, while we were out jogging around the property, two men stepped out of the bushes in front of us. Before I could move, something crashed down on my head from behind and I went down. I was dazed but not out cold; I did not move for fear of getting hit again. I heard the men grab Carman and start away. Because they hadn't searched me for weapons when they started to move away, I was still armed. I rolled on my side and drew my 357 and started shooting. I dropped two of the four but the other two got Carman into the bushes before I could shoot again.

I had trouble getting to my feet but after a couple of tries I made it. I staggered to the bushes where they had taken Carman. When I was through them, I saw the two men lifting Carman over the wall. One of them climbed over. I shot the other one but the one on the other side dragged Carman the rest of the way over before I could get there. I staggered to the wall and climbed over. One man pushed Carman into a car and was getting in behind her. Because I was afraid of hitting her I didn't shoot at him so I shot the driver. The other man climbed over Carman, got out on the driver's side, ran to the driver's door, opened it, dragged the driver out and jumped in. The back door opened and Carman got out and I shot at the driver. I hit him but it didn't kill him. He drove off.

I was a little dizzy so I fell trying to get to Carman. I heard another car coming. I sat up and started reloading my gun. Carman sat down beside me, put her arms around me and told me that she loved me. The car turned out to be the limo with Agent Peterson driving. When he got the car stopped he got out and helped Carman get me into the back seat. He handed Carman a red bandana and told her to hold it on the cut on my head so I wouldn't bleed all over the car. I didn't know I had a cut on my head.

As he drove, be brought us up to date. "The other agents will bring Mahoni and the bags to a new house. Turns out she called your dad to report that you two were getting too cozy and they tracked the phone call. Headquarters instructed you to take their dammed phones away from them. We can't go around cleaning up bodies all over New York. By the way, you shoot pretty well for being conked on the head." I leaned my head on Carman's shoulder and passed out.

When the car stopped I woke up with my head resting on Carman's very nice chest. Agent Peterson and Carman helped me out of the car and up the steps to another house. I hope the FBI has a lot of houses. I was soon sitting in a chair in the kitchen with Agent Peterson sewing up the cut on my head while using nothing to kill the pain. I am a tough guy but I almost passed out again. Carman got a pan of warm water and cleaned the blood out of my hair. While she was cleaning up my head I was thinking of the story of the fish and the bird that fell in love; they had to resolve the question of where they would live. I looked up at her, "If we got married we would have to live in America. Maybe in the northwest where you liked the lakes and mountains."

"Are you applying for the job of my husband?"

"Yes, I love you and don't think I can live without you."

"How would we live? I don't have any money of my own. Do you?"

Agent Peterson, who had been listening, interjected "He's the richest man in the FBI but there is another problem: he is a Jew, not a Palestinian."

She looked shocked. "You have deceived me. Why?"

"I fell in love with you on the plane but I didn't have any hope that you would care for me, so it didn't matter. I thought that when we landed we would go our separate ways and that would be the end of it. I'm not sorry except that you are unhappy."

"I have fallen in love with you, too, but your job application will not be even considered. When all this is over we will have to go our separate ways. And thank you, Mr. Peterson, for saving me from marrying a Jew."

I looked at her for a long minute and then turned and walked out of the house. I was angry at both of them. I turned on my cell phone and called headquarters. When the chief came on the line I said, "I need to be replaced by another agent. Miss Abdula doesn't want a Jew around."

"Who told her you were a Jew? Couldn't you keep that under wraps until this was over?"

"Peterson told her. I guess he thought we were getting too chummy."

"Well, we need you at her dad's hotel anyway since you speak all the languages those rag heads use. I will send someone to get you."

I waited by the gate for a ride. I was feeling pretty low. I knew it had to come out sooner or later, but I wanted to wait until I was more certain of her love for me. When the car got there, I was sitting on the curb with my head in my hands. It still hurt. When the car stopped, I got in and asked the driver, "Who is the agent in charge at the hotel?"

"Gleason. They are not having much luck with getting them talking. Got any ideas?"

"Yeah, do they have bugs in the room?"

"Yes, but they are talking some language other than Arabic."

We were quiet the rest of the way; this guy's name was Gilmore and I didn't like him much. The feeling was mutual.

Gleason was glad to see me. "What happened to you? You look like shit."

"I got beat up by some Jew haters."

"That doesn't narrow the field much. We've got all of the conversation from them on tape, but it isn't in Arabic." I put on the head phones, listened and started writing on a pad what was being said. It was Aramaic, which is another language spoken in Israel. Gleason came over to read over my shoulder as I wrote. I kept fast forwarding the tape and writing. It took a while. They were talking about blowing up something but I couldn't figure out what. Headquarters finally sent a paddy wagon and picked up the lot. They said I could go home and gave me a ride. My bag had been sent to the hotel so it went with me.

Peterson was the driver. "I'm sorry I said anything to Carman. It wasn't my place. She went to her room and didn't even come down for dinner. What are you going to do?"

"Quit. I don't need you guys. Like you said, I have plenty of money and I will find a place to go fishing and maybe write my life story. You're sure to be in it." I was plenty angry with him; he knew I would not say anything good about him. About her, I was just sad, hurt, and disappointed. People not liking you for your ethnicity is just one of those things you have to get used to.

I owned my flat and just paid a maintenance fee on the place. As I entered, the door man handed me a stack of messages. Not one of them was from Carman. In the morning, I took a taxi to headquarters to turn in the resignation that I had typed the night before. Peterson had warned them. The director wanted to see me. He gave me the long speech that they give you for reenlistment. He did a good job, too, but my mind was made up. I cleaned out my desk and went home.

CHAPTER THREE: TO THE WEST

At 0500 there was a knock at the front door. I went with my 357 in my hand, looked through the peep hole and saw a man in a suit with slicked-down black hair but no beard. I opened the door and darted around the corner. Four men with guns came charging in. I started shooting and so did they. I shot straighter. One of their bullets went through my side. I staggered to the door and looked down the hall to see about slicked-down hair, but he was gone and no one else was there. I went back inside and checked the four; one was still alive. I picked up their guns, walked to a table, took the cloth off and laid the guns down. I ripped the cloth and made bandages for my side and tied them on. I took a chair over to the wounded man, sat it down, sat in it and put my foot on his wounded chest and pressed down. I asked in Arabic, "Why did you come to my house?" He put both hands on my foot and tried to move it so I pressed harder. He cried out, "We thought she was here. Is she?"

"No. She found out that I'm a Jew and ran me off." I put in a call to headquarters, told them to send the clean-up crew and that one was wounded and would need a ride to the hospital. Someone in the building had called the cops and they showed up in force. I was about to be put under arrest for shooting a bunch of guys who were breaking into my house when the FBI clean-up crew showed up and rescued me. One of their guys was a medic and patched up my side. I started packing. By the time the clean-up crew was done, I was ready to go. One of the police detectives wanted to know what was going on. I told him to check with the FBI, that they had all the answers. I got my SUV out of storage, loaded up my stuff and headed out. Goodbye, New York.

It was spring. Everything was green and pretty. Driving west, I took 80 west to Davenport then headed north to 90 and turned left. I stopped in a few places to look around. I liked western Montana and drove up around Flat Head Lake looking for a good place to settle. I stayed around for a few days looking at lake front houses but there didn't seem to be anything I liked. I went back to I-90 and on into Idaho. It had a lot of lakes and a lot of houses for sale on those lakes. I looked for two weeks and decided that I needed a ranch with my own lake.

A nice lady out of Sandpoint named Margerita showed me around. I finally settled on a 260 acre place with a six acre lake on it. The owner said that there were some good fish in the lake and that it was deep enough that it didn't kill the fish in the winter time. The house had five bedrooms, each with its own bath. There was a bunk house and two barns. They raised hay and had three tractors and a shed full of other farm equipment. I'm no farmer and I didn't want to be. Margerita said she knew a young couple who could come live in the bunk house and he could do the farming and she could do the housekeeping and cooking. It sounded pretty good to me so she called them. We signed the papers on the place and I wrote her a check. I'm sure she thought it would bounce. It didn't. I stayed in town at a bed and breakfast until the escrow closed on the ranch. I met the young couple and liked them. Their names were Austin and Christine Murphy. I don't know how they felt about Jews but I didn't ask. We went out and looked at the bunk house. It needed some changes to make it livable for a family. Austin said he could do the work so I went to town and opened a charge account at the local lumber company; I told them that Austin and Christine would be signers on it. Trusting, aren't I?

I got permission from the owners to start the remodeling so Austin went right to work. I gave him some money to hold them over until we moved in, then went to town and bought a truck. I opened charge accounts at the local food market and fuel supply. The ranch had fuel tanks by the barn for the equipment and cars.

By the time the escrow closed Austin had the remodel done. Both he and Christine had worked hard to finish on time. I notified the FBI where I was but got a post office box for my mailing address. That is all the information I gave the FBI. We all know you can't trust the government.

When the farmer moved out he took most of his furniture with him. He left two bedroom sets in the guestrooms so at least I had a place to sleep. The Murphys showed up with an old dodge pickup loaded with furniture, pulling a U-Haul trailer behind. And a big dog. I hoped he liked Jews. I drove to Sandpoint to buy a house full of furniture, and some dishes and things. I took Christine with me to pick out kitchen and cleaning things. They delivered the furniture the next day.

The next weekend the Murphys threw a house warming party and invited me. I was impressed that they had so many friends, all nice people. A couple of the guys were carrying guns on their hips. I asked Austin why. "This is north Idaho; there is no law against it here. A lot of people do it." I had to ask him, "Do you?" He answered, "I don't need to. I was in the Marines." So was I but with my training I would feel naked without one.

While Christine got my house in order, I went fishing. Austin started farming. There was an old row boat on the place so I rowed out on the lake and tried out my new fishing gear. It worked. I dropped my cell phone in the lake; I didn't want anyone to find me. When I had enough fish for supper, I went in and had Christine show me how to clean them. We usually ate supper at the big house together. She cooked those fish up perfectly that night. I had the phone company switch the land line phone to the bunk house with an answering machine and notified the FBI that it was a message service only.

Life was good. I jogged around the property, set up a work out room in the barn, helped Austin with the farming when he would let me and fished. I even paid the Fish and Game Department to dump a load of trout in the lake so that I wouldn't run out. Things went like that for a few months. I was happy. When I went to town with a big list for the food store I would pick up the mail at my post office box. One day there was a letter from the FBI. It said that Carman's dad had been killed in a gun battle with another group and that Carman wanted to talk. They must have been tired of paying her bills.

When I got home I called them on the land line. "If Carman wants to talk to me, tell her to call me at this number." Two days later, she called. She was at the Spokane airport and wanted me to come get her. It was about a three hour drive. I told Austin to bring a rifle and follow me in my new Chevy truck. I brought a rifle, too. If we got into a long-range fight we would be ready. As we drove up to the terminal she came out wearing the disguise of an old woman, but she still had eight pieces of luggage. We took off with Austin trailing behind to make sure we were not being followed. As we drove I inquired, "Well, what now?"

"I have nowhere to go. The FBI sent Mahoni back to Israel. My father is dead and I want to be with you."

"I'm still a Jew. You know that hasn't changed."

"I don't care. Do you still want to marry me? I will become a Christian, too; I am very tired of the Muslim rules. We could find a place on a lake and I could run around in a bikini like all the Christian women do and dye my hair back to the original color. What do you say?"

"Do you love me? You know that a marriage needs love, or it won't last."

"Yes, I think that I have loved you from the first but when Peterson told me that you were a Jew the shock was too much for me. I had to get used to the idea. I definitely love you; I really don't care what you are."

"Well, now I'm a north Idaho farmer and I live on a lake so do we need to stop and buy you a bikini on the way home?"

"Yes, and a marriage license." We stopped to eat in Sandpoint at a restaurant with the best pies in the country. Austin ate at a nearby table so he could keep an eye on our backs.   When we got to the top of the hill overlooking the farm I stopped the car, "Do you like the looks of this place?"

"Oh, yes, and it has a lake and a little creek running through it. I love it." She looked at me with a question in her eyes. "Yes, that is our place." When we pulled up to the house, Austin parked beside us and Christine came out of the house. After introductions we all hauled bags into the house. Well, all except Carman. She was running through the house, exploring. We got her bags into my room. When she came in I told her that I would sleep in a guest room; "No. We will start now being married. We can say our vows to each other and do the church thing later. Is there something that I have to do to be a Christian?”

"Yes. Just repeat after me, "Father God, I know that I am a sinner and your son Jesus came and died for my sins. Please forgive me and let me go to heaven with you when I die." She repeated it after me.

"Is that it?"

"Yes, we will go to church and you can learn all about it. We need to go there to arrange for a wedding. Actually, let's go now we can take the Murphys with us and drop them off at the food store."

We left Christine with a long list that Carman had augmented. Austin went to the preacher's house with us. He wasn't a regular church goer but knew the pastor. He introduced us and we were invited in. When we were seated I began the conversation with, "We just bought a ranch here and plan to come to church. Now we would like to get married. She just escaped from back east and arrived today. I'm new here, too. How long does it take to get a license?" "I have copies of the applications here. You could get married today if you had one more witness." He was kidding, but Austin picked up his wife at the food store. We went to the church and were married. You would think that Carman would want a big wedding but she just wanted a quick one.

We didn't even dress up.

On the way home from the church I asked her, "How much more trouble are we going to have with your friends?"

"None, since my father is dead they don't want me anymore. Of course they might still want you for shooting so many of them." Austin inquired from the back seat, "What is that all about?" so we told them the whole story. They didn't quit their jobs; they thought it was exciting.

A long honeymoon started that day; it is still going on. Over the years we have lived in peace. We have four children, three boys and a girl. We go to church almost every Sunday. Carman learned to drive and goes to a ladies' Bible study with Christine. She's getting to be a real American woman.

THE END

LITTLE MIRACLES

CHAPTER ONE

I am a carpenter and builder of custom homes. What I am telling you is a true story. All of my books have been fiction up till now. This one is true.

When this story started my family and I lived in the town of Sebastopol California. We had a five bedroom house on one and a half acres of apples.

We had a horse named Poco Chesta (it means little clown.) We had a dog named Penny. We had a 4 year old son named Eric and a two year old daughter named Sonja.

This all started with my wife Sandy reading a mission magazine. There was a article in it about a Masonry Contractor going to South America to repair mission buildings that were damaged by an earthquake. When I got home from work that night she showed me the article and said, "You could do this." I said, "yes I could, but I don't want to. I have a lot of work right now, If we wait until I run out of houses to build, I would be happy to go then." That wasn't going to fly.

Growing up my father was a Conservative Baptist Minister. I called him and told him what my wife wanted us to do and that I needed the number for their mission board. He thought it was a great idea and said that he would pray for us and would send some money for our support. I didn't think We would need any support because I didn't want to go.

It was a few days before I called the Mission board. The lady that answered turned me over to a man who said that he was in charge of the Africa missions. I think his name was Dr. Baker. He said that my dad had called and told him that I would be calling. He knew my dad. He asked where I thought the Lord was calling me to go? I said, "when the Lord called he didn't mention where he wanted us to go, he just said to call you. So where do you need me the most?" He said, "we have money set aside to build some buildings in the Ivory Coast in west Africa."

I asked how long he thought it would take to do the

work? He said three years. I asked how much support money he thought we would need? He said two thousand a month. We ended up raising seven hundred a month. I had a lot more questions. He had a lot more suggestions.

There was a realtor that went to our church named Richard O'Brian. I went to him and listed my house. I bought a four wheel drive Dodge truck to send to Africa and the mission sent us a list of things to take such as jello pudding and a cassette player and a lot of tapes so we had some music to listen to. We loaded five barrels with things from the list and some from our own list and welded them shut and loaded them in the truck and took off for Huston Texas. Sandy had a brother in law who was pastor of a big church in San Bernardino so we stopped there to see her sister and I spoke at their church asking for support. They didn't like us going to Africa so we didn't get any. We drove on to Arizona to my folks house. Dad was pastor of Tanka Verde Baptist church and I spoke there to get support and we left our dog Penny with them. Dad was real happy that we were going to the mission field. He always wanted to go.

I remember that when we stopped for gas somewhere in west Texas I said, "why don't they give all this sage brush land between here and El Paso back to the Indians?" the man at the gas station said, "they offered but none of the tribes wanted it." The kids started playing a game of who could see something other than sage brush. They would yell, "look there is a house out there." I remember seeing a jack rabbit. The scenery got better after Johnson City. You actually saw a few trees. After dropping off the truck at the shipping Co. in Huston we got on the bus for home. We arrived back in town in time for Thanks Giving dinner with Sandy's family.

The next thing we needed to do was raise support. We went around to churches in the bay area where we had been members and I spoke at their services and told what we were going to Africa to do.

I took our horse to a friend's house. He had ten kids and two other horses so I figured he would get plenty of attention.

Two weeks before we left a friend of mine came over to ask a favor. We had been friends for a long time so I stopped loading my truck to listen.

He said, " I have a chance to bid on a horse arena, but it needs some engineering done and I know that you have one that you use. Would you call him and ask for a truss design for me? The truss needs to span fifty feet and be ten feet on center with purlins."

After making a lot of excuses about not having time, I called my Architect and told him what I needed and went back to moving. The Lord knows what we are going to need, before we need it.

A week later the plans came in the mail and I called my friend. He came right over and I handed him the plans. He spread them out on the hood of my truck which I was loading with the last boxes for storage. He said, "I don't get this stuff. Would you take a look at this and try to explain it to me."

I put the boxes I was carrying in the truck and went to look at the plans. I hadn't looked at them before and they were complicated. So I explained them to him. After going over them for the seventh time I had them memorized.

The Mission board sent us plane tickets to leave on the 18th of December to leave from the Oakland Airport. We were to fly to New York and get a connecting flight that was a direct flight to Abidjon the capitol of the Ivory Coast in west Africa. It was a once a week Pan Am flight.

The church gave us a going away Party and took up an offering to help with the expenses of shipping extra luggage and a bag full of tools. Someone from the church drove us to the airport and the Pastor also came to see us off.

CHAPTER TWO

I had given the Pastor my checkbook so he could send us money if I needed it. He also brought the offering money from the going away party. He was late. He had car trouble on the way. But he made it just as the plane was boarding. He brought enough money to pay for the extra weight for my sea bag full of tools. We prayed and boarded the plane.

The plane ride was uneventful except for Sonia. She had just turned two. The first time she had to go potty Sandy took her. She was so enthralled with the toilet and the funny blue water that she had to go every half hour for the rest of the trip. I had to take her. Now that direct flight to Abijon was a once a week flight. We were supposed to be in New York in plenty of time to make the flight. New York when we arrived was socked in. They flew us around for two hours and finally landed in New Jersey and bussed us to the airport in New York in time for them to tell us that our flight left us behind.

At the Pan Am desk they said, "sorry, but we will put you up at a hotel for the night and fly you to Paris tomorrow and you can change planes there for Africa." As we were crossing the Atlantic I asked God, "we are going over there to work for you, couldn't you get us on that plane yesterday?"

Sometimes you are better off not asking.

When we arrived in Paris we had just 45 minutes to change planes to a Belgium airline. One of our suitcases didn't make it. It was full of shoes.

It was a big rush to get all our luggage over to the other plane in time.

It was a great experience, we watched out of the windows as we flew over the Mediterranean Sea, then over some city on the coast of Africa, then the Sahara with miles of sand and a couple of camel caravans. Some green oasis's and a city all made out of mud. We were flying all the way down the West side of Africa. The kids fell asleep which gave me a break from taking Sonja potty.

The plane stopped in Monrovia Liberia to refuel and restock the food. The stewardess said that we could get off and wait in the terminal, but since the kids were asleep we decided to stay on the plane. Big mistake, when they shut off the engines and opened the doors the temperature went from 68 to 108 in a few minutes.

At the end of the Civil war, America bought Liberia from the local tribes and any of the freed slaves who wanted to were sent there. The buildings look like the old south and the President was a southern Baptist Preacher.

We flew into Abidjon in the dark. There was a Missionary couple there to meet us. When we got our bags we told them we had lost one and they went with us to put in a claim. When we got to customs they wanted to know what was in the sea bag. I told them it was tools. That I was a builder and had come to build some mission buildings. They didn't speak English. A nice man in line told the custom men that they were tools and they let us through.

I don't remember the names of the couple that met us at the airport. They drove us to a mission station there in the city. On the way they asked about our flight. I told them our long sad story about missing our flight. They said, "the Lord was watching over you, the Pam Am flight didn't make it.

It developed engine trouble over the Atlantic and had to land at the first airport they could reach on the African coast. The runway was too short for them to take off loaded so everyone had to be flown out in smaller planes. The first one of them came in today with the news.

In the morning we headed North in a Pugot wagon. The back full of our luggage and the four of us in the back seat. With a kid on each lap for a five hour trip. At least the road was paved. Bouake is the second largest city in the Ivory Coast. It has about 200,000 people. The school is six miles East of town it is also on a paved road.

The school campus is on twenty acres. There are just over a hundred kids and fifty faculty and administrators living there. The kids were mostly gone home for Christmas. Some lived too far away and only went home for the summer. Imagine not seeing your kids for nine months a year.

There was a four plex for single teachers there but it was not finished.

That was to be my first job. We had to stay in one of the dorms until I finished one of the apartments. There were two things that happened the first day there that were unforgettable. Eric was four but tall for his age. He tried to make friends with some of the first graders and they threw him into a thorn bush. The other thing was a meeting of the school board to go over the plans with me of the new buildings that they wanted.

The whole plan was one page of floor plans for a library a movie theater, with a book rebinding room and that was all. I said, "I need more details. How high are the walls and the windows? What is the pitch of the roof?" Doctor Schafer was the head of the Board. He said, "We will decide all of that as we go along. What we want to know is can you design a truss to span fifty feet, to go ten feet on center with purlins in between?" I said, "the Lord provides in advance." Then I told the story of my friend and the horse arena and that I had the plans memorized.

Some of the high school boys came to me and said that I was supposed to give them work to do. The school paid them a few cents an hour. So I put them to work on the first apartment. They had experience working on the buildings so I didn't have to watch them too close.

John Camp was the biggest rascal of the bunch. I asked him, "do the younger kids have to work too?" He said, "they do if they want spending money. Why?" "I need the toughest second grader to do a little job for me. I will pay him. Will you send him to me and don't tell anyone?" He came the next day, I think his name was mike. I told him that I would pay him to come play with Eric and to teach him to ride the bike that I had just bought him. But mostly to keep him from getting thrown into thorn bushes. But don't tell anyone that you are getting paid to baby-sit him. I paid him a dollar a day and he came every day and took good care of Eric.

My wife said, "Isn't Mike a nice boy to come to play with Eric every day." "Yea, it's real sweet of him.

Our first Christmas in one of the dorms.

When we were there about two weeks I came down with Malaria. I was in bed freezing with six blankets over me and it was 110 in the shade.

The nurse wasn't there. When she got back she said, "what kind of preventive medicine are you taking?" I told her and she said, "that's American, it's no good." She gave me some flavocane. Three little pills and I was back to work in three days. I wasn't feeling good yet but I had to get our apartment done before the kids got back and kicked us out of their dorm.

Duane Able, John Camp, and Paul Vandenberg were all seniors and good hands. Between us we got the apartment done and moved in. I built a table and chairs and a couch, and love seat for the front room. We bought some foam and material for cushions for the couches and Sandy borrowed a sewing machine and made covers for them.

Someone gave us a small plastic Christmas tree and

some decorations for it and we pretended to have a merry Christmas in the heat a long way from home and family.

An African cement contractor named Qua May was hired to start on the buildings. This picture is of Qua May and one of his workers working on the four plex. The next is of John Camp.

On a trip into town to the hardware store a young fellow told me in English that he needed a job and that his name was Esaka. He was a native of Ghana an English colony. His English wasn't real good but he spoke good French and a couple of native dialects. I hired him as a laborer for two dollars a day and used him as my French teacher and translator. Translators got eight dollars a day. Esaka spread the word that I needed carpenters. About twenty showed up. All but one had just a hammer in the way of tools. One fellow had a tool box full of tools, him I kept.

He turned out to be a good hand. I put him and Esaka working on the four plex. When I wanted something I would yell Esaka he would answer, "yes master." I would say, "I am not your master." He would say, "Yes you hired me so you are my master." That went on every time I needed him. He was a real likeable kid.

One day I went to pick up a board off a lumber pile and a little voice behind me said, "Don't touch that board."

I looked around there was nobody there. I took out my hammer and lifted the board with the claw. There was a puff Adder under there ready to strike. If it had bitten me I would have had a slow painful death. I've often wondered who it was that warned me. There seemed to be a lot of small miracles happening over there. They only have one type of pipe over there. It's the grey stuff that we use for electrical. It takes a special kind of glue that they don't sell over there. Their glue takes three days to dry. I had sent a letter home asking the home church to send me the right kind of glue whenever they thought of us.

I was doing some plumbing in one of the apartments and I used up the last of the glue that we had when Paul came in and said, "The main water line to the school just broke. I need the glue to fix it." I said, "I just used the last of it there isn't even a drop left." He said, "There are a hundred and fifty people here. In this heat we are all going to be smelling bad in a big hurry."

I said, "ask God to send you some, Paul he's probably listening." He bowed his head and asked God for some glue and just then a guy from the office came to the door and said, "there is a package for you at the office." Yea it was glue. Ten thousand miles from the hardware store and the glue gets there right when you need it. Oh yea it's just a coincident.

Missionaries bringing their kids back from Christmas vacation came to meet us. And look over what we had done to the four plex. They all asked "where did you get the couch and the big chair." I told them that I made them. They asked if I would make them some. The only furniture you could buy in the stores were made in France and were very expensive. The high school boys dorm had a wood shop in the basement. I helped them set it up to make some furniture and the girls sewed the cushions. I figured what was the cost for each piece and set the price so that the kids could make a profit to split up between them. The word spread and the kids got busy right away.

Word came that the ship bringing our truck had reached Abidjon.

The business manager for the school, Dennis Grudda told us that he would have to go with us to get everything through customs. We took the train down. The whole family went along. Sandy wanted to do some shopping in the big city.

It took a week to jump through all the hoops and sixteen hundred dollars for duty and bribes to get the truck released. When we drove out of the shipping company's yard the business manager said to drop him at the train station to get a ride home. I said, "if you don't mind riding five hours with a kid on your lap you can ride with us." He did, it was a good thing. We would probably have had a hard time finding our way out of town without him.

We stopped at a supply depot and picked up some cases of canned goods for the school. On the way north we stopped at a mission of the Christian Missionary Alliance group and had lunch with Joe Ost and his wife. We went to a French restaurant. After we ordered Joe stood up and started preying in French very loud. He thanked god for our food and then preached a salvation message to the French people. I looked around to see how the French people were taking it. They all had their heads bowed and their eyes closed being very respectful. Joe was a big guy from Alaska I think they thought it was a good idea to be respectful. When he sat down he apologized but said this is probably the only time these folks will hear the story of Jesus. What a guy.

CHAPTER THREE

When the four plex was about done I started making cabinets for a mission station in Abidjon. I worked from measurements sent to me. The cement contractor had finished making the block for the new buildings and started laying them. It would take some time so we loaded up the cabinets and headed for the big city. Dwayne Able and John Camp went with me.

It was getting late when we got there so we unloaded the cabinets into the apartment and went to the mission station where we were to stay. The lady who ran it had went to bible school with my mom and dad. After dinner at the mission the boys talked me into going ice skating at the big hotel. I didn't know how to ice skate but it was cold in there. Probably the only cold place in west Africa.

I started learning to skate. Duane met a French girl and spent the whole evening skating with her. He had a girl up north that he was planning to marry when he got out of school that summer. She was a thousand miles away. And the French girl was cute. She invited us to her folk's house for dinner the next night. I was to go as chaperone. I hadn't learned much French yet so I just sat there like a dummy while everyone talked away. She met us at the skate rink every night. The apartment wasn't square so we had to remake the cabinets and the counter tops and it took a few days.

It was over a hundred degrees and muggy so we cooled off at the skating rink every night. We met some men from Lebonon who spoke some English. Nice fellows. John Camp slept most of the way back and Duane talked about his two girl friends. He was excited because the one up north was coming to spend the weekend at the school in two weeks. She had graduated the year before and was looking forward to seeing him and her other friends. So for five hours I had to listen to how great it would be to see the American girl and when we take the next set of cabinets down he will see his little French girl for a few days.

After listening to it for a while I started thinking up a plan. When we arrived back at the school I told John Camp about it. He loved it. He sat down and started writing. I told him what to say. He wrote it in French, having grown up there he could write it like a native. He took it to my wife.

She had very nice handwriting. He told her it was to a friend in Abijon. She couldn't read French so she couldn't give it away. He put it in an envelope and addressed it to Duane with a Abidjon return address. Two days later I asked Duane to go to town with me to get some lumber. On the way back to the school I stopped at the post office for the mail. I slipped the letter into the pile on the way back to the truck and handed the pile to him when I got to the truck.

There was always a pile of mail with all the people at the school. As I drove Duane sorted through the mail and found his letter. He said, "hey look a letter from that girl in Abidjon." He was excited. He started reading. He yelled, " OH NO she says she is coming up here next weekend." I said, "what's wrong with that? Your folks will be glad to meet her." He said, "that's the same weekend my girl from up north will be here. What am I going to do?" I said, "you will figure something out."

"She says her father is a contractor and is coming to bid on a job here and if he gets it she will come stay with him for the summer."

"Don't worry you'll be gone back to the states." When we got to the school Duane came to my apartment with me to see if I could help him think of some way for him to get out of his problem. John Camp came over and Duane told him the whole sad story. John said, "You should just get on your motor cycle and ride out to some native village and camp out for the weekend." We were having a lot fun with this. While Duane and I were in town, John had told the whole school about it and soon Duane's brother showed up. He came in and listened to Duane's sad story. He said, "John Camp told everyone all about it while you were in town."

"But how could he know? I got the letter in town."

"He knew because he and Uncle john here wrote the letter." It was too funny. We both started laughing. John jumped up and ran out of the house laughing. Duane and his brother glared at me and walked out. My wife who had been standing there feeling sorry for Duane looked at me and said,

"you are an ass. If you worked at your job as hard as you do fooling around we could go home sooner."

By this time the four plex was finished. I was busy making tables and chairs and couches for them and doing the finish electric and plumbing jobs. The cement men had laid two layers of block in the new building and was ready for the wiring. Here you just laid the wire on the block and left a loop of wire sticking out where you wanted a outlet. Light switches came later.

Every day a new snake came to inspect the work that was going on. Most of them were poisonous. In one week there were three cobras a green mamba, an African Beauty snake, a green tree snake, and a rock python.

The high school boys kept the python as a pet.

Two of the African workers came to me one day and asked, "what are these different groups of missionaries?

Here we are Christian, Moslem, or spirit worshiper but here you have conservative Baptists, CMA, Southern Baptist, Jehovah Witness, and a couple of Pentecostal groups too." I said, "well, you two are of the Baoules tribe, That fellow over there is a Senoufo, those two are from Upper Volta, I don't know what tribe that is, but you are all Africans. We are all Christians just different tribes." That worked for them. The gospel according to Brickwedel.

The block layers finished the walls on the library and movie theater building and started on a house for a family. I did the rough plumbing and started building the trusses for the big building. I was building them up on top of the walls. A fifty foot truss is too heavy to lift up there when it's done.

One day I was up there working when the dorm parent

for the second grade boys dorm came by and said that he had seen a big green snake stick it's head up from under the side walk in front of the dorm. He asked if I would take a look and see if I could figure how to get rid of it? He had a flash light and showed me the spot. The hole was about eighteen inches wide and six high and went way down out of sight. I couldn't see anything down there. How was I going to catch a snake I couldn't even see? I got an idea, I went to some dorms and borrowed some mouse traps and lined them across the mouth of the hole and went back to work. An hour later I went to check on my traps, they were all popped. I reset them and went back to work. Two more times I reset them and then here comes a banged up Green Mamba down the middle of the street. He was getting out of Dodge. One of the boys took a two by four and had a little talk with it. I don't know why every time someone sees a snake they call me.

We loaded up the last load of cabinets for the apartments in Abidjon and John Camp, Duane Able, and I took them down and put them in. John was in a bad mood all the way back. I asked, "what's eating you?" He said, "it's all these rules. Who wants to be a Christian if you have to go by all these rules?" I said, "When I got out of the marines I was playing tennis with the youth pastor from our church and he asked me, "why aren't you a Christian?" I said, "I don't like the rules you Christians have to go by." He said, "what rules?" I said, "thou shall not go to dances, or movies, or drink, or smoke, or kiss the girls. I like all those things and life would be pretty dull without them." He said, "those are Pharisee rules. Jesus didn't like them either. He made fun of the Pharisees for making up extra rules that's what those extra rules are like. The Bible says to work out your own salvation. That means to make a deal with God. Like, I would like to be a Christian, but I would like to keep dancing and going to movies and kissing the girls. God will think it's fine. Those are not his rules." John was angry because his girlfriend didn't want to have sex. I said, "you are going home in a month, when you get there, no more rules."

The Principal of the school, Mr. Ragsdale said that the school dinning hall had bats in the roof. Could I get rid of them? I told one of the boys to drill a few two inch holes in the highest part of the gable end of the roof. Then they plugged up the holes under the corrugated roofing. We waited a few days until the bats got used to using the drilled holes to go in and out then I stripped the insulation off of some wire and tacked the two bare wires across the holes and plugged in the other end. Electricity there is single wire two twenty. The next morning we had a wheel barrow full of dead bats. Every morning we had dead bats for about four days. When the bats quit dying we covered the holes with a rest in piece sign.

During the rest of the school year the boys could only work for a few hours a day and Saturdays. So I did most of the work. When school got out we all turned to.

One night the School nurse sent word that there was a snake going up her screen door. I rounded up the night watchman and went on another snake hunt. The night watchman had a battle lantern, a spear, and a machete. When we arrived we didn't see any snakes. But he knew where to look. He found the snake wrapped up in a bush. He handed me the lantern and took a swing at the bush with his machete and ran. The cobra came out of the bush fast and hooded up ready to fight. There I was just standing there with the light on it. It was spitting venom at me and I backed away. I motioned for the watchman to hand me his spear with which

I hit the snake and stunned it then the watchman stepped in and chopped off it's head with his machete.

The next day I asked the school business manager,

"how many snake bites have you had there at the school?" He said, "in sixteen years we have been here we have only had one. One of the high school girls was walking to her dorm at night and stepped on what she thought was a stick that flipped up and hit her in the leg. When she went into the dorm, the dorm mother said she wanted to talk to her for a minute. So they sat down and had a cup of coffee and talked. The next morning the girls leg hurt and she realized that she had been bitten. She told them where she had been hit and they found the snake still there. They knew that the only antidote for that poison was caffeine. She said that she didn't normally drink coffee, but since the dorm mother asked her to, she had. Those kids played hide and seek at night out there and no one died. Someone was watching.

By the end of summer all the buildings were finished and they wanted my apartment. We loaded up the truck and headed North for Ferkessedougou. The mission had a hospital there that needed some work. By this time I had learned enough French to get along without an interpreter.

Esaka stayed at the school, he was a good worker and they used him as a maintenance man. The first job at the hospital was to fix the water system. They had two wells but lightning had struck the tower on one and knocked out the pump. So the whole hospital was running on one well. An American construction company had just finished a sugar refinery near there and they were selling off all of the stuff they had left over. Dr Shafer and I took the truck over and bought a water tower and hauled it back and the crew and I set it up by the second well. We had also bought a new pump.

I climbed down into the well and hooked up the pump. They had built a du-plex for single nurses that I had to finish and it needed to be hooked up to the water system too. I was climbing up a concrete water tower made out of block. It had blocks turned sideways for a latter. As I reached for the next block a little voice behind me said, "don't put your hand in there." I didn't need to look behind me to see who was talking, I was too far off the ground for there to be anyone there. I stepped up one step and leaned out to see what was in that block. It was a standard viper. They are only about a foot long but if they bite you it only takes a minute for it to kill you. I took out my hammer and pushed it out the other side of the block. I yelled down to one of the African workers down below that a snake was coming down. He made short work if it. Another little miracle. I still wonder whose voice it was warning me.

Dr. Schafer had two horses and wanted to know if I knew how to train them? Well I was from out west. Even though I had lived in a city most of my life. One of the horses was a two year old stallion. That was the one he wanted trained. I got him so you could ride him but you had carry a stick in your hand or he would reach around and try to bight you. While we were at an African Market I saw that the booths had short whips for sale. I told Sandy that I would like to have one for dealing with that horse. She is the kind of shopper that has to go from shop to shop to check the quality and prices on an object before buying it. After a couple of shops we got a following of men watching her and talking in African and laughing. I got tired of it and asked, "what is so funny?" One of them asked if my wife spoke French? I said, "no why?" he said, "what are you buying a whip for?" I said, "I am training a horse that is lacking in discipline. The whip is for him." He said, "we don't have horses here because of the sleeping sickness." "Then why are so many whips for sale?" "For our wives. We didn't know white men beat their wives too." "Some should. But in my country it's against the law." "Well the big joke is, is she trying to find a soft one so it won't hurt so much?" The crowd grew and more jokes and laughter until Sandy turned to me and asked, "what is so funny?" "Those whips are for beating your wife. They want to know if you are trying to find a soft one so it won't hurt so much. Or one with just the right shape to leave marks the way you like them." She said,

"buy your own whip." And walked away. I told the group what she said and they walked away laughing.

A Gabon viper was next to the house one morning. A African worker saw it and killed it.

They had a nice little two bedroom house for us there

with a large screened in porch. Someone felt sorry for us because we didn't have any pets and gave us a grey African parrot. Cage and all. You fed them palm oil nuts. He would eat the outside then spit the seed out. Not in his cage, through the bars of the cage onto the floor. He was raised on the back porch with the peoples dog. It didn't talk it growled and barked. Every morning at daylight it would go through all the local bird songs. After putting up with that bird for a couple of months I gave it to some African boys who hung around all the time. I don't know what they did with it.

Samuel and his sister. They lived a thousand miles north near Timbuctu. Their father was a blacksmith. Samuel got T.B. and got to the place where he couldn't walk anymore so his dad loaded him on his back and took the twelve year old sister along to do the cooking and they walked down to the hospital. It was only a thousand miles.

Samuel would never walk again so I built him a self propelled wheel chair. You petal with your hands.

CHAPTER FOUR

A French doctor named Wolga and his wife and daughter came to work at the hospital. His wife Michele didn't speak any English. It was arraigned for my wife to watch their little girl until noon each day. Nadine was the same age as Sonja. I would be home for lunch when the lady came to pick up the little girl. Sandy and Michele would talk back and forth neither one understanding the other. Sitting at the table on the screened in porch I would be eating my lunch trying not to laugh. Once in a while it would go quiet. I would look up and they were both staring at me. One of them had asked a question and I was expected to translate. I would listen to the question, translate it translate the answer, and they would go back to talking again. This went on every day.

One day an African boy named Karim who was twelve came to me and said, "the doctor lady told me to follow you around and correct your French when ever you made a mistake." The next day I told her that I am a carpenter not a pastor. My French does not need to be good. She said, "it is not good for a French person to have to listen to your bad grammar."

I was riding my moped with a tool box on the back and rode that around from job to job. We had a dozen workers working all over the hospital grounds. One day as I rode up to where four men were digging a ditch my motor quit. On those old mopeds you had to take out the spark plugs and clean them when they quit. I was doing that when an old woman came walking up. She had on a long skirt and no top and no shoes. She had a long staff and started tapping it on the ground and dancing a slow shuffle. Mumbling some thing. All the African workers took off. Karim was hiding around the corner. He said, "that is a witch and she's putting a curse on you. I said go get Tourna. He was the only Christian on the crew. He came walking up and said, "Yea, boss what do you want?" I said, "the kid says that that old lady is a witch and is putting a curse on me. Is it a bad curse?"

He listens for a minute and said, "no just that you will fall in a ditch and break a leg or some thing." "Why did all the men run away?" "They were afraid some of the curse would splash over on them." "Why aren't you afraid?" "I'm a Christian and her old curse can't bother me." "Tell her that I'm a Christian too and tell her that I am going to count to ten and then make the ground so hot she won't be able to walk on it." Then I went one two and she took off running. He said, "can you do that?" "No but she don't know it."

The word spread and the next couple of weeks the workers walked way around me. And Karim started going to the Baptist church in town. If a Christian could scare a witch he wanted to know more about it.

The elders of the Baptist church in town came to me and asked, "can you help us with a project we are working on?" "Sure, what is it?" "We have built some apartments for visiting African Pastors but they need a roof and we don't know how to build it." I went and looked at the project. It was just three rooms about twelve by twelve each. I figured up what it would take to do the roof and gave them the list and kept one for me. I went to see the Doctors and told them about the project. Dr. Shafer said, "we are not going to let you do it. You are here to work for us not for the Africans."

I said, "I notice that the missionaries all take a month off every year and wonder around and visit the other missionaries. I have been here for over a year and a half and haven't had a day off yet. I'm taking a week off." He said, "they don't have enough money to do the job anyway." I said, "I have a hundred dollars in tithe money I will put in..

Doctor Dilinger said, "I have two hundred." Dr. Shafer said, "oh so do I." I said, "if you guys don't like Africans what are you doing here? Couldn't you get jobs in the states?"

I went and helped the African church put a roof on their building. I liked the Africans and like most people if you like them they will like you.

Dr. Slater's son came to me one day and said, "I saw a cobra go under a piece of tin roofing in our back yard. If you would hold the tin up I will get dad's shotgun and shoot it. I found a long stick and when he was ready with the gun I lifted up the tin. There were two snakes under there he shot one and the other one took off. He shot at the other one, but only wounded it. Then the gun jammed. The snake then turned to fight. It hooded up and started blowing venom at me since I was sword fighting with it with my stick to keep it around to kill it. The Dr. came out and took the gun from his son and shot the snake.

The girl with her hand missing has Epilepsy. Every

hut has a fire in the middle of it. It's to cook on and keep the bugs out. When in one of her fits her hand fell into the fire and her mom couldn't pull her out because they believe that she has an evil spirit and if she touches her it will come into her. They had to take off the hand at the hospital.

An African Pastor told me that to do some evangelistic work during the week he would pick out a trail that led into the jungle and get on his bike and ride out. There was always a village at the end of a trail. This time he rode out of the jungle into a clearing and saw a group of kids playing. As he rode closer they saw him and turned and ran into the village. Almost immediately a group of men armed with spears and bows came out to meet him. The chief asked,

"did you just come in here on that trail?" He said, "yes, why?"

"Because normally when anyone comes down that trail there is a lot of howling and screaming goes on and the person comes out of the jungle in a big hurry. Are you a witch or something?" "I told him that I was a Christian and those spirits didn't have any power over me." They wanted that kind of power. We sat down in the shade and I told them how to get that power and they excepted the Lord. The Chief declared the village a Christian village.

I know that it sounds strange but he makes the whole

village line up and say the prayer that the Pastor tells them to say, he makes the men build a church and a parsonage and hires a Pastor from the seminary in Korogo. Then he makes everybody go to church. Eventually it is a Christian village.

Anybody who doesn't want to go along can move away.

We arrived in Africa at the end of a four year drought. One quarter of the population of Mali the country to the north of us, died from lack of water.

Some Mennonite missionaries shipped over a well drilling rig and made a deal with the government to provide the well casings, hand pumps, and pipe. They went around drilling wells at the villages where their hand dug wells were drying up. When the new wells were producing, the elders of the village would come to the drillers and ask, "what do we owe you?" "Just ask your village to come listen to a story.

Then the Chief would usually declare the village a Christian village and it would become one. Sooner or later. We heard that a Christian village of two hundred people was attacked by eight thousand Moslem raiders riding in off the desert. They surrounded the village and then about a hundred of them would jump on their camels and ride toward the village firing their muskets, yelling and waving their swards.

The musket balls wouldn't go through the thick dried

mud walls so the defenders just stayed down until the raiders started riding away and then they would raise up and fire back. The battle lasted six days and four people were killed.

Then the army got there with a jeep and two soldiers.

One driving and one manning a machine gun mounted on the back. They fired a long burst over the heads of the Moslems and the raiders all jumped on their camels and rode off into the desert. The end of the battle.

Well I finished all the work that they could think of for me to do so I sold my truck to a local garage to use for a wrecker and we had a yard sale and sold a lot of clothes and all of my tools and got ready to leave. The African workers had a going away party for us. They brought all of their families and laid out a big picnic lunch under the trees. They sang songs and played games. It was very nice. The missionaries had one too. I told a story about a little trouble I had selling my truck. I told it in my much improved French because some people there didn't speak English. When I was done I turned to the French Doctor's wife and said, "how did I do?" She said, "very good John." When Dr. Dilinger drove us to the train the next day he said, we were all impressed with the going away party that the workers gave you. I been here twenty years and that was the first one they ever gave.

I said, "if you like them they like you. You guys need

to be nicer to them. How do you expect to win anybody to the Lord if they don't like you.

The train ride to Abidjon was interesting. Some places the train had to slow down to ten miles an hour because the tracks were bad. We stayed overnight at the mission station in town and went to the airport the next day. The plane left at eleven at night. It was ninety four degrees.

When we landed in Brussels it was thirty seven and snowing. We didn't have any warm clothing. We had the cab drop us off at a department store and bought warm shoes and clothing. We took the train to France. On the way through Switzerland we had to change trains at Bearn. Our luggage was checked through so we kept an eye on it. When the train left that we were supposed to be on, our bags were still sitting on the platform. I went to a baggage handler working there and told him that our bags had been left behind. And that we would stay there for a few days if we could have our bags.

He understood my French but answered me in German that he couldn't let us have our bags but that his boss would be back in a few minutes and that he could. I went and told my wife what he said and she said, "you talked to him in French and he answered in German. How do you know what he said?" I said, "Hogan's Heroes." We spent some time running around Switzerland before we went Home.

To you people who read this book, and are not Christians, you will probably not believe these stories. I feel sorry for you. You think it's hot in Africa, wait until you get to hell. Thank you for listening.

THE END

www.ingramcontent.com/pod-product-compliance
Lightning Source LLC
Chambersburg PA
CBHW040517170726
48295CB00012B/230